*June*

Copyright © 2014 by Reverend Jen Miller
All rights reserved.

Published by Art Star Scene Press

First Printing: December 2014

Cover photo by Ann Enzminger Bronshav
Cover and book design by Marie Mundaca

# June

### Reverend Jen

**ASSP**
ART STAR SCENE PRESS

Every man is a fetishist. You simply have to discover his fetish.

> Anton LaVey

## Chapter 1

## *Might Try to Break the Rules*

Scarlet handed me the file for my first client, Pete—forty-nine years old, five-foot-seven and two-hundred-and-forty pounds.

Upon hiring me, Dylan quickly dispelled the notion that S&M scenesters are a hip-looking crowd. "Most of your clients will look like the father on *Family Ties* with a furrowed brow and guilty look," she said.

Going over Pete's file, I noticed he had few preferences regarding clothing and activities. Clients rated fetishes on a scale of one to five, with five being most preferred. Gloves were the only item marked off and they only rated a four. At the top of Pete's file, someone had scrawled, "Might Try To Break The Rules" in bold letters. This warning, coupled with Pete's obvious contempt for clothing led me to believe that he would try to sway me into breaking a cardinal rule—*I was not allowed to remove my underwear.*

*What the hell do I wear?* I wondered. Gloves, obviously, but what else? I pulled on a turquoise g-string, a tight, black slip and black patent leather opera gloves. Black stilettos and Wet-n-Wild "Wet Red" lipstick completed the look.

Scarlet peered into the dressing room. "June, when you're

ready, will you please lead Pete into the Medical Room?" For my session with Pete, I'd been given a choice of either the Medieval Room or the Medical Room. I chose the Medical Room because it looked like something out of *Barbarella* whereas the Medieval Room had gloomy Renaissance Fair décor. Plus the Medical Room housed two alien masks that Doms wore when torturing men who had alien abduction fantasies. Hence the Medical Room was the silliest of The Inferno's five rooms.

Pete stood sweating at the end of the corridor.

"Hi, Pete. I'm June," I said, shaking his hand. Had Scarlet told him this was my first time? I hoped not.

I led him to the Medical Room. We stepped in and I closed the door. He looked me over, smiled and took a seat.

"We need a safe word," he said. "Pick a color."

"Violet," I said, and then thought, what a stupid safe word. Who wants to utter three syllables when they're in pain? But I could hardly change it, as Pete certainly wasn't paying me to recite the contents of a box of Crayola.

He told me to go outside, get some matches, wipe off my lipstick and take off my heels.

Stepping outside I tried to wipe off the lipstick, but since it was Wet-n-Wild it stained like most cheap lipsticks. Grabbing some matches and removing my heels, I returned.

Pete then ordered me to slowly remove my gloves and lay them at his feet, which I did, smoothing them out neatly on the floor.

"Stand up and face me," he said.

Standing up, I turned to face him. He lifted his hand in the air and slapped me across the face.

My natural reaction when someone slaps me is to slap back, but I managed to refrain. He continued to slap me on the face and I couldn't help thinking he slapped like a girl. I started to smile.

Center stage of the Medical Room sat a white leather gynecology table with straps and stirrups hanging off it.

"Bend over the table," he said.

I bent over and he pulled my slip up, revealing my turquoise thong. I had never worn thong underwear before. In fact, I'd always made fun of thongs, calling them "butt-floss" and wondering why anyone would want an all-day wedgie, but Scarlet said thongs were popular with clients. I'm assuming this is because they look trashy. No matter what you do, you really can't dress up a thong. Also thongs leave the ass cheeks bare and vulnerable.

Pulling my slip up a bit more he began to caress my ass with his pudgy little hands. Then the spanking began. Since my ass is the fattest part of my body, it wasn't too painful. The spanking continued for some time until he instructed me to stand up and face him again. He slapped me a few more times before delving into my personal life.

"Where are you from?" he asked.

"The Lower East Side."

"What do you do?"

"I'm a writer."

"What do you write about?"

"Animals."

"How old are you?"

"23."

"Do you have a Master?"

"Yes." (A lie. Technically, Stuart was my *lover*, not my *Master*. But Pete didn't want to hear about that, I'm sure.)

"Were you with your Master last night?"

"Yes," I said, becoming aroused at the memory.

"Did you suck your Master off last night?"

"Yes."

He slapped me again, this time harder than before.

"Bend over."

He pulled my slip all the way up, revealing the sheet burns on my spine.

"What are these?" he asked.

"They're sheet burns. I got them from fucking my Master for an extended period of time."

"Do you love him?"

"Yes."

"Does he love you?"

"Yes." (Another lie. Stu only told me he loved me when drunk, but to mention this would have opened a whole can of worms that Pete could not have been ready for.)

"Take off your slip," he ordered.

Peeling my slip off, I wore only the thong.

Pete then stripped down to his boxer shorts.

"Kneel at my feet," he instructed.

Once I was down on my knees, he began to interrogate me. I didn't listen to a word he was saying, a skill I picked up in high school lab science class.

He ordered me to then get up and lie down on the table. *All this getting up and lying down is exhausting,* I thought. As I lay down, he fastened the table's straps around my wrists. My feet were free to kick and swing.

"Have you ever had hot wax?" he whispered.

"No," I said, revealing my newness to the profession.

He scurried off and returned with a set of mammoth nipple clamps, which he clamped onto my tiny breasts. The clamps hurt, but I breathed deeply, trying not to fidget.

I stared into the mirrored ceiling and began to study myself. I still had tan lines and the thong was pushed down so low my pubic hair was almost visible.

"Close your eyes," he said.

While pretending to close my eyes, I glimpsed Pete stroking his cock through the opening in his boxers while simultaneously lighting a candle. Though his multitasking impressed me, I wondered if he was going to remove the clamps before he gave me the hot wax.

He returned with a lit candle.

"Have you ever been spit on?" he asked.

"No."

Leaning in close, he spit, aiming for my breasts.

A globule landed on my clamp-clad right nipple. He spit again, aiming for the left. He rubbed the spit into my chest, which made the skin feel tight.

"You might have a lover, but I'll make you my bitch," he said.

Who was he kidding? The truth was I was too disinterested for him to claim me as his bitch. I stared in the mirror some more. I looked like a victim in a sci-fi film. The blue in my eyes matched my thong.

In the mirror, I watched Pete lift the candle and tip it toward my breasts. He poured the hot wax over them and I screamed, more from shock than pain. He began drizzling hot wax over my entire body, finally bringing the candle near my face.

"Please, not my face," I begged, not wanting my eyeballs seared.

To my surprise, I started to cry. The nipple clamps felt tighter. My skin was blistering hot from the wax. The tears ran between my lips. They tasted like cheap shampoo and raindrops.

Pete unfastened the wrist straps and pulled away. "Touch yourself," he said.

Slipping my hand under my thong, I was surprised to find the material soaked with wetness. I was turned on but had no idea why.

"Are you wet?" Pete asked.

"Yes," I moaned, inserting two fingers.

But just as I was starting to have fun, Pete interrupted me.

"Get off the bed and kneel at my feet," he demanded.

Kneeling on the cold floor I shivered as he removed his boxers, revealing his tiny, erect penis.

"Will you touch my balls?"

"No. It's against the rules."

"You can wear a glove," he insisted, as if a small layer of latex would make the act legal.

Still it was my first session and I didn't want to argue. He handed me two latex gloves, a small one that was too tight and a big one that was too loose. Timidly I touched his balls and then stopped, insisting I just couldn't bend the rules.

Undeterred, he told me to get back on the table and put my feet in the stirrups. Once my feet were in the stirrups, he spanked the back of my thighs before lifting my legs in the air and instructing me to keep them there. *At least my abs are getting a workout,* I thought.

"I'm a switchover," he abruptly stated. "Do you know what that means?" Without waiting for an answer, he continued, "I see Mistresses and Submissives. The Mistresses here like to fuck my ass with dildos. Would you do that for me?"

"Sure," I agreed, and then quickly thought, W*HAT am I doing?* But a deal's a deal and before I had to time to think of a way out, he'd laid out three dildos, draped in condoms and ready to go. He told me to start with the small one and move up to the fat one. The fat dildo was…like no human penis on Earth. It was monstrous. Pete reclined on the table as I'd done moments before, with his chunky legs and feet in the stirrups. Slathering the smallest dildo in K-Y, I inserted it. It slid in so easily that I was shocked. While I worked it in and out, he yanked on his penis.

"Do you do this to your lover?" he asked.

"Occasionally, with a strap-on." (Yet another lie. I'd only done it once with a strap-on.)

"Does he like it?" he asked. "Does he like to get fucked in the ass?"

"I guess so."

"Has he ever fucked a man?"

"Yeah, once, but he didn't like it. I mean, his body liked it, but he didn't like that it was a man. He's confused."

"Do you think he'd like to fuck me?" he asked.

"Sure. Maybe." This was an outright lie. Pete and I both knew the truth—no, he wouldn't.

"What does your lover look like?"

"Well, he's tall and has long brown hair, tattoos, green eyes and strong arms."

I was on the brink of going into details about his cock when I suddenly felt sorry for Pete. This is why I will never be a Dominatrix. I *know* Pete wanted to feel like crap, but I'm just too good at that game—making men feel like crap.

Pete was hardly listening anyway, as he was so carried away that he was now yelling, "Fuck me! Fuck me!" and ordering me to fuck him with the giant dildo. The giant dildo slid in just as easily as the small one. It was like watching a sword swallower at work. It just didn't seem anatomically possible. He stroked his penis with abandon until a small spurt of semen came out.

After a moment of uncomfortable silence, I produced a roll of paper towels and a spray bottle of alcohol. He cleaned himself up while I peeled hot wax off my skin.

Finally we were both dressed. Pete handed me a fifty-dollar tip, which combined with the eighty-five dollar cut from the house, made for a decent payday. (Astonishingly low given what I'd just endured, but more than I'd ever been paid for anything.)

"We'll have to do this again," he said.

I wasn't sure I could.

## Chapter 2

## *An Ass Made for Spanking*

It was 1995 and I'd just quit my job working at Paco's, a Mexican bar and restaurant in New York's East Village. Mostly, I worked the register and took phone orders, but on weekends the sadistic owners insisted I stand in the middle of the sidewalk handing out brochures while wearing a massive taco costume. Despite the fact that no one could see my face, the humiliation was almost unbearable. For starters, the East Village was then teeming with hip, beautiful people—models, musicians and artists. Plus, the taco costume looked more like a giant vagina than any kind of taco. The "pink meat" center looked like Georgia O'Keefe had designed it. Add to this the fact that half the East Village seemed to be tripping on acid, and you have a recipe for disaster. After being continually poked, prodded, laughed at, abused and even worshiped as a pagan idol, I peeled off my taco getup and told the boss to kiss my grits. Surely, I could do something else.

Unfortunately, Paco's was just one in a long list of hell jobs involving low pay and humiliating costumes. I'd only been out of college a year, but already I'd been a costumed Transformer robot at FAO Schwartz, a clown-wig-wearing face painter in Central Park and a Disney Princess at a child's birthday party. (Belle, in case you were wondering.)

I looked for office work, but my résumé was clearly that of a person who is too insane to get a normal job and too sane to get disability.

I had no savings, no trust fund and no marketable skills. Thanks to my art school education, I could tell you how many times a day Picasso pissed, but I couldn't add, subtract, type, copyedit or do any of the things temp agencies hire people to do. The first of the month was approaching and I needed rent money or else I would lose my rent-stabilized apartment on Manhattan's Lower East Side. Rolling pennies and hosting an open mike in a rundown art-hole were just not cutting it in terms of a financial plan.

My friend, Dylan, the frontwoman for a goth metal band who also did performance art wherein she simulated knifing her vagina onstage, suggested I could make some money at the dungeon where she worked.

In case you've never looked at the back of a *Village Voice*, a "dungeon" (sometimes called an S&M/Fetish Parlor) is a place where men and women (mostly men) pay hundreds of dollars so that people called Dominatrices will beat and/or humiliate them. Sometimes the men and women (again, mostly men) pay hundreds of dollars so they can beat others. These unfortunate beating recipients are called Submissives.

Dylan thought I'd make a great submissive. I was 23, had a gamine's body, few morals, no money, a writer's curiosity and "an ass made for spanking" according to her. (She'd actually spanked my ass one night after a show when we were both particularly drunk and randy.)

The dungeon where she worked was called The Inferno. Located in midtown Manhattan, it had a reputation as the most lavish in the city. She'd been there for almost a year, ever since my best friend, Kyle, had broken up with her. Their relationship had been full of Master and Slave scenarios, bondage, role-play and lots of regular old boning. When Kyle broke her heart she resolved to "get paid" for what she'd been doing so well all along. Now after months of submissive work, she had decided to become a Dominatrix since she'd grown tired of "being beaten" and "swatting penises away." This left an opening for me.

Dylan introduced me to Richard and Clarissa, the married couple who owned The Inferno. At the time, I looked about 15, wore my brown hair in a chin-length bob and almost never wore makeup. I was a tomboy who was more comfortable on a skateboard than in high heels. Dylan had told them I "kind of looked like Joan of Arc."

The first thing Richard said when he saw me was, "She really does look like Joan of Arc! We ought to get her a stake!"

The first thing Clarissa said to me was, "How old are you? You don't look 18."

I told her I was 23 and even though I had no experience in the sex industry and very little experience with BDSM, Richard and Clarissa agreed with Dylan that I would make a good Submissive. They offered me the job, which I accepted without hesitation. Though the sex industry scared me, the thought of eviction scared me more.

I was about to go from being a slave to The Man at Paco's to being an actual slave in a dungeon. As far as I was concerned, the two were hardly different. Either way I was an oppressed worker reinforcing and perpetuating an exploitative capitalistic scheme. And at least at the dungeon, I'd be making a hell of a lot more money. So it was with this kooky Marxist notion in mind that I entered into the sex industry.

The best way I can describe what suddenly "entering into the sex industry" is like is to compare it to the TV show, *Land of the Lost*. If you remember that scene in the opening credits where the Marshall Family fall through a dimensional portal and end up in a strange world full of dinosaurs and Sleestaks, you'll have some idea of what it's like. It's a shock at first— being thrust into an alternate universe that is often unsavory and at times downright treacherous. But, like the Marshall family, you've got to survive so you learn to navigate your way around. Pretty soon, you're used to it.

The strange world of the sex industry isn't something I discuss too often even though I've been *trying* to write this book for years. But every time I started, after a few thousand words, I'd always feel overwhelmed. So I'd stop and write something fun. I knew that writing this book would *not* be fun. It would be *work* and I hate work. (Clearly, since at one point I chose to take beatings in a dungeon rather than go to work like a normal person.)

Most people who've worked in the sex industry put a lot of effort into trying to *forget* the shit they endured. By writing about the shit I endured, I'd be *trying* to remember. I wasn't sure I wanted to. I wasn't sure I *could.* After all, my dungeon days coincided with my early twenties so my memories are shrouded in a practically opaque veil of booze and nonstop partying. If it wasn't for my journals, I'm not sure *I'd* even know I worked in a dungeon. And as for my journal entries, they're sporadic. After a session at the dungeon, I usually reacted by trying to erase what had just happened with alcohol. Sometimes I'd write something that had nothing to do with what had just happened– plays involving unicorns and talking animals.

Only occasionally did I painstakingly write about what had transpired. It never occurred to me at the time that someday I'd want to write about my experiences. Now that I am, it's these detailed journal entries that are serving as the book's framework along with other tales of bohemian extremism—escapades that happened outside of the dungeon, but which are no less debauched. Of course, bohemian life and the sex industry have always gone hand in hand for at least as long as theater and opera have existed.

A few things you should know about bohemian life at the end of 1995 in New York City. Mayor Giuliani's "Quality of Life Campaign" had just gotten underway. It was aimed mostly at ruining the quality of life of the poor and artistic while improving the quality of life of the rich and conservative. As a result, almost every square inch of Manhattan had become unaffordable with few exceptions. One exception was the Lower East Side, which had yet to be totally gentrified. (Gentrification can be defined as making an unprosperous neighborhood prosperous or as making a once-rockin' neighborhood suck.) At the time, the Lower East Side was still unprosperous and as a result it still rocked. Because rents there were relatively inexpensive, it's where I was living, in a squalid 6-floor walkup tenement I shared with a gay photographer/performance artist/writer/maitre d' named Jake. Together, we barely made ends meet, possibly because we went out every night. Though we both aspired to be artists, we spent more time drinking, smoking and screwing (an assortment of crazies) than we did creating. If I'd bothered to spend half as much time painting and writing as I did partying, I'd probably have a mid-career survey at the Whitney today. But making art is solitary. When you're young, energetic and beautiful, it's almost a waste to do so. For two years, Jake claimed to be writing a one-person show about George Washington Carver, but I never saw a word of it. I actually did put on a couple of one-person shows —poorly attended, disorganized events wherein I read stories about my life directly off the paper while barely noticing the audience.

Jake and I were also part of the thriving open mike scene that had taken root on the Lower East Side. Jake hosted a weekly open mike at a hotel in midtown and I hosted a monthly open mike at a theater around the corner from our apartment. Most of our friends were other open mike regulars—poets, performance artists, playwrights, aspiring authors, comedians, freaks and other ne'er do wells.

It was pre-Bush, pre-Cheney, pre-9-11, and pre-Iraq War and it was pretty damn fun, this pre-millennial era when people could still smoke in bars and people still met in bars because they weren't holed up in their apartments writing status updates on Facebook. Not that the nineties weren't just as rife with tragedy as any other decade; there just seemed to be a little more freedom. People were less careful about what they said, less suspicious, less fearful. On the Lower East Side, our biggest fears revolved around being bored or running out of beer. Beyond that, not a whole lot else seemed to matter.

Hopefully this gives some context for what my life was like during the roughly two years in which I stepped in and out of the sex industry with the finesse of *Angel– Honor Student by Day/Hollywood Hooker by Night.* As I mentioned earlier, back then it never occurred to me that someday I'd like to write a book about the dungeon, partly because I didn't think of myself as a writer yet, and partly because there seemed to be an excess of books about the sex industry. I wasn't sure the world needed another one. Now that I am a published author, I still don't necessarily think of myself as a writer. (I'm more like a performance artist masquerading as a writer.) And I'm still not sure another "sex industry book" is needed. What I *do* know is that a lot of books about the sex industry have an angle, or even worse, a moral, and if there's one thing I hate, even more than work, it's a moral. (Even worse, some of them hardly have any sex!)

So what I've attempted to do here is just tell some stories because I can't do much else. There's no moral. No lesson to be learned. I didn't find God or get sober. I didn't get married and have children. I didn't become a nun or a normal. My life is almost exactly the same as it was back then only now I don't work in a dungeon. And I don't regret anything I've done.

I have no angle here. I'm not out to enlighten or educate you. In fact, you should probably do the opposite of everything I do in this book. (Except for practicing safe sex; you should always practice safe sex.) I'm also not out to turn you on though you might find some of these stories arousing. You might even find them jackable. You might even wanna run out before reading any further and pick up a Costco amount of tissues and an economy-sized bottle of lube just in case. But that's not my intention. All I want is for you to keep reading.

## Chapter 3

## *You're Gonna Be Fine*

"A lot of girls get hired here and they think it's gonna be like *Story of O,* all glamorous and sexy," Dylan said, casually spraying down a leather bed with cleaning fluid. The place reeked of rubbing alcohol and cigarettes.

"But this isn't *Story of O,*" she continued. "No one here is doing it for love. You might get off on it sometimes, but it's a lot different than doing it for love."

"What's Icy Hot doing here?" I asked, pointing to a jar of it in one of the glass cabinets.

"Some guys like to rub it on their balls. Whatever you do, don't ever let them rub it on your pussy."

I made a mental note.

The Inferno was like nothing I'd ever seen before. There were several rooms, each a different theme, each with innumerable implements of torture. There was a giant wheel upon which slaves could be strapped down and spun *Price is Right* style. Penis-shaped wall hooks held hundreds of coils of rope. There were human-sized birdcages and leather masks displayed on mannequin heads. There was a medieval-looking chair with a dildo protruding from the seat, which apparently wasn't enough because the chair could also be operated, by a crank, to shoot from floor to ceiling. There was a schoolroom with a chalkboard, desk and table. There were two medieval style dungeons. There was a mirrored medical "examination" room and a baroque room with soft fluffy carpeting, gilded mirrors and a gold throne.

My mouth was agape as Dylan gave me a tour.

We stood in the middle of the medical room and she looked me over like a bad girl in a Linda Blair "women in prison" movie. Her long, unnaturally bright red hair had short Bettie Page-style bangs and her lips were carefully painted red. Her tiny waist was cinched together with an intricate ribbon-laced bustier. How would I ever get into such complicated clothing? At the time, I'd never owned any fetish gear. About the only thing I ever laced were my Converse high tops and even those were sloppily undone half the time.

"Have you ever been suspended?" she asked.

"No," I answered, embarrassed by my lack of experience.

"You should try everything before you start. It'll make you more comfortable."

She motioned me toward the suspension bar.

I let her take my wrists and cuff them to the bar, which she raised using a nearby crank. Slowly I was elevated until my toes dangled off the ground. She tickled me lightly.

"Do you know what a cane feels like?"

"No." All I knew about canes is that they were used to severely punish graffitists and shoplifters in far off lands.

"You don't ever *have* to agree to be caned. Personally, I

can only take five or six at a time, but if you can take it you'll get good tips."

I took a deep breath as my ass involuntarily clenched in expectation of the cane.

"I won't do it too hard," she promised. "Relax."

I tried to relax, but it was sort of like waiting for a shot at the doctor's office. I knew pain was on the horizon. She chose a cane from a basket of them and smacked my ass lightly with it. The sensation wasn't a thump; it was a sting, like instantaneous sunburn.

She leaned in close to me and kissed me on the cheek.

"You'll be fine," she promised.

*I would be fine,* I told myself. I only planned on working there until I got some money together and then I would quit and do something else. Maybe I would join a convent or work at Kmart. Maybe I would do some normal thing like become a UPS Man, which I suppose wouldn't be that normal if I were to become a UPS *Man.* I would become a UPS *Person.* Delivering boxes in the same brown uniform every day there would be no room for eccentricity except for when it rained and then I would put on my flashy, yellow official UPS poncho. I would get medical and dental and vacation days and everything would be really and truly fine.

But for now I'd have to do some very strange shit.

When my orientation was finished, Dylan told me to come back the following afternoon and to bring something like a schoolgirl uniform and some lingerie. She said I could borrow her fancy fetish gear until I was able to afford my own and reminded me to bring some ID. "Gotta make sure you're legal," she said.

Walking back to the Lower East Side at twilight, I stopped briefly at "Bunnie's", a children's clothing store where I acquired a crisp white shirt and navy blue tie to go with the Catholic schoolgirl mini-kilt already in my closet. From there I wandered down Ludlow Street, dropping into Barramundi, a watering hole my friends and I went to as often as Janet, Jack and Chrissy frequented the Regal Beagle. (In fact, we'd begun referring to Barramundi as the Regal Beagle.)

Not surprisingly, I found Kyle there, bellied up to the bar, sipping a three-dollar "hapless hour" pint, sporting some new purple streaks in his otherwise dark hair.

"Hey, dude," I said, sliding my still-stinging ass onto a barstool.

"BFF! What's going on?"

"Not much. I'm digging the purple. Is that Just for Men or L'oreal Preference?"

"Manic Panic. I did it last night. Now my pillow's all purple."

"The price of beauty is too high."

Kyle dyed his hair weekly. It was, as he put it, a "superficial reaction" to "deeper problems." Why go to a therapist when you can just dye your hair?

"How was The Inferno?"

"Well, the name is appropriate because I'm pretty sure I visited a circle of Hell today. I think it's the circle that people go to when they desperately need rent money."

"Alice, you're like the only person I know who has never worked in the sex industry. I hate that you're doing this."

Kyle was especially bitter toward the sex industry, having just quit a job as MC at the Exotic Angel Cabaret where many of our friends worked. When I asked him what he hated most about the club, he told me it was "watching amazingly talented women perform stunning routines and then seeing these wealthy, clown-mouth, dickheads ignore the tip jar before dropping sixty bucks on the 'pretty girls' in the lap dance room. " It was an experience he summed up as "fucking gross."

But I was already tired of people, dudes in particular, acting as if I had a ton of other options. I'd *tried* to get other jobs, but no one would hire me.

"Kyle, if you can think of a way to make my rent money magically appear I'd love to hear it."

"I'd almost rather you rob banks or something."

"Maybe the big check will come tomorrow. I *know* this is the year I'm gonna win Publisher's Clearing House."

"Ed McMahon would never get that check up your stairs."

Kyle, a chain-smoker, enjoyed complaining about my six-floor walkup.

"I'm also gonna devote myself to regularly playing lotto, but you have to remind me to buy the tickets. I've got a dollar and a dream, but a horrible short term memory."

"Speaking of which, someone actually won fifty bucks playing scratch-off at the check cashing place today. I'm convinced the world is gonna end because *nothing* happy has ever happened there."

"That is clearly a sign of the apocalypse. Maybe I should start smoking again." I'd only quit smoking three weeks earlier. Looking around The Inferno, I realized the likelihood of me starting again was great. There were ashtrays everywhere, all of them overflowing. Dungeon employees appeared to smoke even more than doctors.

"I've smoked a pack already today and I'm on my third pint. I need to slow down, but I've been worrying about you all day."

"Don't worry about me. Please. Just get Lucille's attention because I need a pint of Pilsner immediately."

Lucille was busy mixing a bunch of complicated drinks for some normals at the end of the bar— three dudes who looked like they worked on Wall Street. This was a new phenomenon— guys in khakis coming to the Lower East Side for fun. Because these individuals tended to wear striped rugby shirts (even though most of them had probably never played rugby), Kyle and I had taken to calling them "Stripe Shirts."

When Lucille was finished serving the Stripe Shirts, Kyle flagged her over to us. "Hi, Alice. Pilsner?" she asked. She had a cheeky smile, a British accent and ample cleavage— three things that ensured her success as a New York City bartender.

"Yes, please."

The Pilsner Urquell was perfect, crisp and cold. It was by far my favorite beer though I was hardly a beer snob. If a beverage at the bodega had a big, orange sale sticker on it, I tended to buy it.

"So how is Dylan?" Kyle asked.

"Smoking a lot of weed, even more than normal. She misses you, but she has so much pride she'll never admit it."

"I feel like she's trying to get revenge against me by getting you all mixed up in the sex industry. She knows how much I love you and the easiest way to hurt me would be to hurt you."

"Dylan was getting revenge against you when she got *herself* mixed up in the sex industry. She's getting me a job, which is more than I can say for most people."

At that point, Lucille did a shot of booze and breathed onto a match. Fire shot out of her mouth. The Stripe Shirts applauded and ordered a round of shots. Neither Kyle nor I batted an eyelash.

"This is what worries me. We're becoming totally numb to the surreal," he said.

I thought of the penis wall hooks.

He continued, "It sounds so stupid because it's not like you're a virgin. I know you're not *innocent*, but I still don't want you to lose your innocence. I don't want you to hate people."

"Too late for that!"

"Good point."

"And *innocence* is a complicated word. There are almost as many definitions for innocence as there are for love. As long as I'm not hurting anyone, I see no harm in gaining a little more worldly experience, shedding some innocence for knowledge."

"You ever think maybe you'll be hurting yourself? Maybe

you'll be hurting the people who love you and don't wanna think of you tied up with some gross dude slobbering all over you?"

"I hurt myself all the time. I drink a case of beer a week! And, seriously, Kyle, I am only gonna do this for a little while."

"You do realize that's exactly what people in the midst of heroin addiction say when they first try it?"

"Is the Public Service Announcement over? If it is, I'd like to go back to talking trash and drinking beer with my BFF."

"I'm shutting up."

"*I am going to be fine, Kyle.* Trust me."

"I trust you. It's everyone else I'm worried about."

## Chapter 4
## *Down the Rabbit Hole*

When I started at The Inferno, I was told to choose a pseudonym, one that would entice clients to hire me. After careful deliberation I chose "June." It was fittingly innocent, given my "barely legal" looks at the time. Plus, it was a nod to Henry Miller's second wife who must've been a masochist to marry the bastard.

In the sea of exotic pseudonyms my coworkers chose, *June* stood out. There was Constantine, Natasha, Jade, Alexandra, Isabelle, Nikita and Anastasia. These women were, for the most part, bad-ass-looking, busty, tall and heavily made up. They could pull off these names. I could not. I did not look like a Constantine. I *look* like an Alice. I *am* an Alice, like Alice in Wonderland or the druggie teen in *Go Ask Alice* or even the waitress on the show *Alice*. And I'm sort of a combination of all three—part naïve and curious, part impulsive and self-destructive and part wisecracking and independent. Almost like Multiple Personality Disorder but all my personalities are Alice. I am constantly fighting with myself. The independent part hates the self-destructive part and they're all doomed because of the curious part. Curiosity killed the cat and it's almost killed me a few times. My mother tells me I was named after Alice from *Alice's*

*Adventures in Wonderland,* which is appropriate because I've always felt there must be a saner world on the other side of the looking glass if only I could figure out how to get there. Problem is, no one ever hands you a map to a saner world possibly because none exists. If you look for one you just fall further down the rabbit hole and into the depths of insanity until you end up at a place with penis-shaped wall hooks. This is what's called "having no direction." And it is in my directionless quest that I gave up Alice and became June (at least for the few hours a week I spent at the dungeon.)

*June* was a terrific marketing tool—one powerful syllable that reeked of pearls, white gloves, goodness and prudishness. June—a spring day, an all American name, reminiscent of *Leave it to Beaver*—June Cleaver—gagged and covered in hot wax, in pumps and corset or maybe high-heeled Mary-Janes and bobby socks. Clients got a throbbing boner before they even walked in the door or saw my picture, just hearing that name. And I knew exactly what I was doing by choosing it. I targeted the men who were looking to consume innocence, to spew their gobs of jizz allover the American dream. And it worked like a charm. It was as if I'd just tossed a bucket of bloody chum into shark-infested waters. Men appeared in droves, champing at the bit for a taste of my rotten cherry pie.

Aside from Pete the sword swallower, most were forgettable—guys in suits with martini-halitosis who tied me up and spanked me while trying to convince me to touch their penises. A lot of time at the dungeon was actually spent lounging in the break-room, where girls could nap, read, gossip and smoke while awaiting prospective clients. Some of the girls had beepers so they could leave and come back if beeped when a regular showed. (This was in the old millennium, pre-cell phones!) But in the beginning, I had no regulars. Being, in the break-room, gussied up and ready for action at all times was the only way I would get them. Some guys would only visit once, driven there by curiosity. Others were slaves to whatever fetish obsessed them. These were the guys you wanted because they were almost guaranteed to return.

I was lounging in the break-room reading Iceberg Slim's *Pimp* when a first-time client named "Dave" arrived, requesting a submissive. Since I was the only girl doing strictly submissive work, I was offered the session by default.

"A couple of things though," Scarlet warned me, "First, he's got really bad psoriasis all over his body. It's not contagious, but it might freak you out."

Though I'd only worked at The Inferno for a couple of weeks, I was pretty sure nothing could freak me out.

"Also, he's kind of a prick."

"I guess it wouldn't hurt to talk to him."

Scarlet dealt with these men all day. Most didn't score very high in the charm department. I wondered what one had to do to be defined as a "prick" by her.

"His name is Dave and he's sitting in the waiting room. And, seriously, you don't have to see him if you don't want to. He said you could just wear street clothes."

Most clients wanted me to wear my schoolgirl uniform or trashy lingerie. Street clothes might have been the most unusual request yet.

I found Dave in the private waiting room, which was a lot like a doctor's waiting room, only instead of *Highlights* and *National Geographic*, clients could read *Vault* and *Black and Blue Magazine* while they waited. These were the fetish magazines that dungeons advertised in. (Pre-internet-boom, they were essential.) Because I looked so young, Richard didn't want me to appear in the ads, which he thought might arouse the scrutiny of the 5-0. This was fine with me since part of me still believed I might someday be America's Sweetheart and appearing bound and gagged in a glossy could thwart this from happening. Instead, clients could see my picture in the big book of "staff photos" Scarlet and Frankie (the other receptionist) kept behind the front desk. Since I didn't do a photo shoot until several weeks after being hired, the book contained exactly one photo of me—fully clothed and playing the flute in front of the fake forest scenery at Kmart Portrait Studio. Scarlet was convinced this was actually more arousing to my client-base than real fetish gear. (She was busy earning a Ph.D. in philosophy and full of brilliant insights.)

I introduced myself to Dave.

He immediately told me about his psoriasis and pulled up a sleeve of his shirt so I could see it—red, splotchy, bumpy skin. It looked painful.

"It's not contagious," he said.

"I know."

"So, it doesn't bother you?"

"No."

"Good."

It didn't bother me. If anything I felt sorry for him.

Dave chose the "Versailles" Room, a luxurious albeit cheesy baroque space decorated in blue and gold. Gilded mirrors stood alongside cupid-shaped fountains. A gold armoire held gold bondage masks, riding crops and taffeta gowns, which were popular with the cross-dressers. The back wall of the Versailles Room rotated into one of the medieval rooms, like the walls of a haunted mansion on *Scooby Doo*. It was a secret that only employees were privy to, just in case you had to escape a lunatic. In all, the Versailles Room kind of looked like the living room of an eccentric Long Island family. My pet name for it was the "Quelle Fromage Room." At the center of Quelle Fromage sat a large gold throne. Across from it hung a huge mirror and in between the throne and mirror stood two Corinthian pillars outfitted with wrist and ankle straps, the idea being that the submissive who was bound to the pillars could gaze at their countenance *or* they might be bound with their rear to the mirror, giving the Dom two views at once.

Music played an important part in each session, not just because it created ambience but also because CDs made it easy to time a session without wearing a watch or if you were blindfolded. I popped in a Mozart CD someone had left in the room. I knew nothing about classical music except that this particular CD lasted about 50 minutes.

Dave then told me to fetch a collar from one of the phallic wall-hooks and to put it on. I did, noticing in the surrounding mirrors how incongruous it looked with my jeans and rainbow-striped tank top.

"Now the way I understand it," he said, "is I can do anything I want to you as long as it doesn't exceed your limits and you can't take off your underwear and you can't rub my dick to make me come."

*Dick,* I thought, *is the least erotic word in the English language.*

"That's pretty much how it works."

"I can say whatever I want and you won't cry?" he asked.

"I never cry," I said, quoting Alice Cooper though Dave hardly seemed like an Alice Cooper fan.

He instructed me to kneel at his feet. The soft, baby blue carpeting of the Versailles Room was nicer than the cold floor in the Medical Room. Affixing a leash to my collar, he led me to the foot of the throne.

He sat down in the throne and began barking commands. He really was, kind of a prick.

"Kneel with your head down. I don't want you looking up. You look up and I'll blindfold you."

As I knelt before him, his hands wandered over the seat of my jeans until he began smacking my ass, first with his hand then with a riding crop. This was followed by quietude.

"Get up," he finally said.

When I stood up I saw that he had stripped down to nothing but a flimsy, dirty t-shirt. His chest, arms and legs were covered in flaking red rashes that looked itchy like poison ivy. It was heartbreaking. He had a smallish penis that was just beginning to rise. But it wasn't the psoriasis or the dirty t-shirt or the smallish penis that bothered me; it was the fact that he wore a smug expression that reminded me of every scary cop I've ever seen. I pictured him sitting in a cop car outside of McDonald's eating a Big Mac with special sauce dripping down his chin.

"Why are you so nervous?" he asked, sensing my jitters.

"I'm always nervous with someone new," I said. Really I was nervous because he looked like a cop. He was new to The Inferno so there was no file on him. Richard was paranoid about the po-po and this translated to a general paranoia amongst the staff. Although I hadn't done anything illegal, I imagined that what he would really get off on was beating me for real, handcuffing me for real, taking me into the station and ruining my life just for kicks.

He ran the riding crop over my shirt and my nipples perked up.

"I like it that you're nervous. If you weren't nervous, you wouldn't be a good submissive."

He slipped the riding crop under my shirt. It was cool and soft. He smacked my breasts lightly then ran the crop over my jeans and thrust it between my legs. He moved it around, and the movement coupled with my sadistic cop fantasy made me wet.

"Now, I want you to touch my cock."

*Here we go—here come the cuffs, I* thought. He handed me two latex gloves. Putting them on, I touched his cock for a millisecond. I didn't like touching his penis, but my adrenaline rose thinking maybe I'd find myself in jail that evening, licking the vulva of someone who considered me her ho. Maybe I'd finally get on TV via an episode of *Scared Straight*.

"Get down on all fours and kiss my feet," he demanded.

Once on all fours, I noticed the little hairs on his toes and the Neanderthal length of his toenails. He could've hung like a sloth from a tree from them. I breathed through my mouth so I wouldn't have to smell his feet as I kissed them. My red lipstick left traces across his feet while Alice Cooper ran softly through my head—*Take away, take away my eyes. Sometimes I'd rather be blind. Break a heart, break a heart of stone...*

My mantra was interrupted as Dave got up and told me to follow on all fours. He walked quickly so I could barely keep up. Finally he reclined on a rickety gold ottoman, leaving me on my knees, which were now burning from the carpet.

"Kiss my feet. And this time, I want to feel your tongue."

I ran my tongue over his foot, licking and kissing it like it was salvation, hoping he would come so I could get the fuck out of there.

He then told me to stand up and face him. When I did, he used the riding crop to push my zipper down. Shoving the riding crop inside my pants, he worked it between my thighs. He lifted my shirt and sucked on my nipples.

"Take your shirt off."

I removed my shirt and he pulled my nipples toward him, putting a pink, plastic clothespin on each one. (If you have sensitive nipples and want it to appear as though you are in pain in order to please your partner, but don't actually *enjoy* nipple torture, always go for plastic as opposed to wood. It's less painful.)

He yanked my pants down, revealing my pink, thong underwear from Kmart.

"Do you know why you're a whore?" he whispered.

"No." This, I imagined, was the proper response for it allowed him to elaborate on the various reasons why I am a whore.

He pulled on my underwear. "Because of this," he said.

He licked my breasts and pulled on my clothespin-clad nipples. "Because of this," he repeated. "Whose breasts are these?" he asked.

"They're mine, Sir," I said, knowing this would result in punishment. He smacked my ass with the crop.

"They're yours, Sir," I said.

"That's better, *whore*."

He fondled my ass.

"I bet a whore like you loves to suck cock. Why don't you suck me off?"

"I'm sorry, Sir. You know the rules."

He pulled me across his lap so that I was dangerously close to his penis. If he were a cop, he was certainly enjoying himself. He began to spank me while begging me to take off my underwear, offering me more money to do so. His obsession with me going bottomless fueled my neurotic fear that he might be a cop. Day one Scarlet had explained the "rules" to me.

"No hand jobs or blowjobs," she said. "Of course, if he's a client you've seen a bunch of times and he tips well, you could give him a hand job but just wear latex gloves and use your discretion. You can go topless but you *cannot* go bottomless though again, if he's a regular, use your discretion."

Since Dave was new I refused to go bottomless although it took all the strength I could muster since I could've used the cash.

"Look, I've only got ten minutes left, so why don't you just suck my cock?"

"I can't, Sir."

At that, he took my hand and placed it on his crotch. I refused to move it so he thrust his hand over mine and moved my hand up and down his shaft until it throbbed. I imagined explaining this at court—*I didn't jerk him off. He jerked himself off using my hand.*

I was fondly reminded of the many times my older siblings had taken my hand and made me smack myself in the face with it, all while taunting, "Stop smacking yourself! Stop smacking yourself!" Could explain my masochism.

My self-analysis was suddenly interrupted as Dave announced, "I can take care of this now. Get down and kiss my feet and I better feel your tongue,"

Once I was on all fours, I thrust my ass in the air and kissed his feet, worshipping his toes with such fervor that I didn't even see him come, just heard the incessant moaning and then the quiet that followed. Looking up, I saw that his stomach was covered in cum.

"June, right?" he asked.

"Yeah."

"June's not your real name, is it? You'll probably never tell me your real name."

"Of course not."

"What's a nice girl like you doing in a place like this?"

"I only *look* like a nice girl."

"Well, June, you're really either a great professional or a true submissive."

## Chapter 5

## Own It

Had Dave been right? Was I a true submissive? I certainly wasn't a great professional or even a decent actress. But there was no denying one simple fact—my pussy was wet after every session, even if I spent most of the hour wishing the session would end, even if the guy were gross, even if I was painfully tired, hungry or cranky. Maybe my vagina was trying to tell me something my brain wouldn't admit to—that I liked being dominated.

There were girls at the dungeon who were *Lifestyle Doms*. They practiced their trade at home with their lovers, went to fetish events and fully embraced the fetish lifestyle. Some of the Doms were actually *lifestyle subs* who switched roles once they got home. And then there were girls who were just trying to make a buck, put themselves through college or simply keep a roof over their heads. Though I'd experimented with some wild sex acts (the aforementioned fucking my lover with a strap-on) I'd originally thought myself the latter. I imagined my stint at the dungeon would be like a mafia hit—in and out and nobody gets hurt. The possibility that I might physically enjoy it hardly occurred to me. And here I was *physically* enjoying it. Here I was being a superfreak! This terrified me. Life was confusing and complicated enough. I didn't want to try living it in a latex mask.

I'd always enjoyed a little caveman action in the sack, being held down and having my hair pulled. I liked feeling "taken" probably because my self-esteem was so low; it thrilled me that anyone would bother to take me. Clarissa once explained to me that submission is essentially narcissistic. So much of it boils down to, "Don't I look awesome in these handcuffs?"

Being *paid* to look awesome in handcuffs was especially gratifying even if it was coupled with licking hairy toes and being called a whore. I'd long ago stopped thinking of "whore" as an insult. Whores were women so desirable they got *paid*. They were also women who chose to do something completely outside of what society deemed acceptable. To be a whore was therefore the ultimate act of rebellion. It was also a dividing line. Working in the sex industry, you realized there were two types of people—those who saw whores as beautiful outlaws, and those who thought a whore was the worst thing a person could be.

Because my circle of friends was comprised solely of bohemian freaks, I didn't run into many haters. Most friends were fascinated, not judgmental. But Stuart, my lover of two years, was far from thrilled. He thought there were girls who did "that kind of thing" and girls who didn't. He couldn't wrap his head around me, a girl who'd come to New York on a scholarship at age 17, taking her clothes off for money. What he didn't realize is that most of the women at The Inferno were educated (albeit in totally unusable fields of study.)

On a practical level, Stu was concerned about my safety despite the revolving walls, intercom system and screening process. On a purely visceral level, he was repulsed by the idea of other men touching me despite the fact that he and I had an open relationship. And I use the word "relationship" loosely. Stu was a musician and I had yet to realize that believing a musician can be a good boyfriend is like believing in unicorns—it's just something you have to grow out of. He was barely employed but he hardly had time for me anymore. He'd gone from wanting to sleep with me every night to biweekly midnight booty calls. I figured he was screwing other women, but we had a *Don't Ask Don't Tell* arrangement so I could only guess. Jake, my roommate was struggling through a similar situation with his "boyfriend." At one point, we changed our answering machine's outgoing message to– *Hi, this is Alice and Jake. If you are calling after 10 p.m., please call back during regular business hours to schedule an activity or date with us.* We wanted to go on dates like normal people even though we were far from normal. And I was getting further from normal every day.

Meanwhile, Kyle had a new girlfriend with a squeaky voice and perky tits named Jessica. He was now happily boning her thrice daily while I was desperately lonely for my best friend. Jessica therefore became "Jessicunt" the woman who had stolen my friend with her vagina.

I found myself spending more and more time at the dungeon trying to nab clients and the more hours I spent there, the more I hung out with Dylan. Often we'd sneak into The Inferno's bathroom together and smoke weed, stuffing a towel at the base of the door like we were in a college dorm. Stoned, sessions were much funnier than sober. Occasionally, we did sessions together where Dylan dominated me along with one of her clients. It was win-win because we both got paid and we got to keep each other company. She also went easy on me, never spanking or whipping me too hard. Afterward, we'd go to the yuppie bar downstairs and feast on bar food and beer, rubbing elbows with people who'd probably never handled dildos and riding crops in their lives.

At the bar, I shared with Dylan my conflicting emotions about being part of the sex industry. On the one hand, I did admire sex workers. They *were* rebels against the idea that all women had to be perfect Madonnas. I also liked having free time to make art, something my shitty restaurant and retail jobs hadn't afforded me. But I felt a somewhat unfamiliar emotion creeping in—*shame*. Each time I rang The Inferno's buzzer to be let upstairs, I was sure every single person in the Flatiron District knew I was about to do some freaky shit and that my pussy would be absolutely soaking wet afterward. And I was sure that, even if I said nothing to my family, they would somehow figure out what I was doing and disown me. I would become the family embarrassment, the subject of terrible gossip in my little hometown in Delaware. My mother would never be able to go to the grocery store again.

I'd been properly loved, fed, housed and parented yet somehow I'd ended up working as a sex slave. I told my parents I was "temping" which they bought despite the fact that I had no skills. I guess they figured anyone could answer phones and push papers around. But I knew it would kill them if they ever found out. I also knew they would loan me money if I asked for it, but I couldn't bring myself to ask. My parents weren't poor but they weren't rich either. I'd chosen the fucked up, unstable life of an artist—I'd made my bed and now I had to lie in it (naked and possibly in chains.) Maybe I was, in fact, addicted to martyrdom. Or maybe I was just trying to figure out who I really was, exploring my masochistic side and my darkest sexual fantasies. Twenty-somethings do all kinds of crazy shit to find themselves. And it wasn't like I'd joined a cult or taken out exorbitant student loans to go back to school; I was profiting from my self-exploration. Still I was ashamed that my self-exploration was so steeped in perversity.

"Here's how I look at it," Dylan said, "You just have to *own* it."

Dylan was the queen of *owning it*. Her band even printed up "I Love Whores" t-shirts, which she proudly wore, usually with a pair of hot pants so short she almost had ass cleavage. She was only two years older than me but she made me feel like a child, an asexual, uncool child.

She continued, "You're a writer so *write* about it. Get up at your open mike and talk about it. We get to see things other people don't. Think of it as *material*. And don't forget, whatever guilt you feel about working at the dungeon, your clients feel it double. At the end of the session, they feel so guilty they're *happy* to give you money. So take it. Take as much of it as you can get."

## Chapter 6

## *At the Chelsea Hotel*

Despite Dylan's advice, I hardly wrote about the dungeon. Instead, I made lists.

1. A cane was broken across my ass by a man from Argentina.
2. Played a witch today, being persecuted in 1666. (I chose the year.) Had a possible past-life regression.
3. I wore a ball-gag today. They aren't made for mouths as small as mine. Cuffs don't come in my size either.
4. Pretended to be a kitten for a client. Did lots of meowing and purring and when I curled up, I almost fell asleep.
5. So much spanking. Being punished for imaginary transgressions.

I figured I would fill in the details later, but things moved so fast I never did. What I know is that up until I met Annie, I behaved. I had barely broken the rules or plunged into the abyss.

Annie was my first pimp.

I'd heard the myths and legends of Annie, of her overwhelming fondness for pain and her ability to "take" a session harder than any submissive out there. She got pierced with long needles, burned with cigarettes, beaten mercilessly and she loved it! Those were the tall tales of the fabulous Annie. I'd seen her picture in fetish magazines that lay about the waiting area. She had long blond hair that naturally fell over one eye a la Veronica Lake, big brown eyes, pouty lips, a petite yet curvaceous figure and a proud look on her face that said, "Nothing will ever shame me." For a submissive, there seemed to be no vulnerability. Dylan told me that Annie was a lesbian and a lifestyle sub who had worked at The Inferno as "Penelope" for a couple of years, but had gotten in a fight with Richard and quit shortly before I arrived. Now she was a free agent.

I'd been working at The Inferno for about three months when Dylan introduced me to Annie one night at a party. We hit it off and she asked me if I'd do a private session with her and one of her regulars at the Chelsea Hotel where she lived. I agreed to do it for one very simple reason—*money*. At The Inferno, Richard and Clarissa took approximately seventy percent of what clients paid to see me. With Annie, I would be paid five hundred dollars for the hour and I wouldn't have to hand over one cent of it. My rent was then only four hundred and fifty dollars a month. The idea that I could pay my rent in an hour thrilled me.

Arriving at Annie's hotel room, I didn't know what to expect, but felt quite fearful for my ass. If the stories were true, I knew it would not leave her premises until it was thoroughly battered.

She answered the door in her underwear, eating a piece of fruit, seemingly oblivious to the fact that our session was about to begin. I'd never been in a room at the Chelsea before and somehow expected it to look bohemian, messy and antique. Instead, everything was black, white, silver and immaculate. It almost had a retro '80s *American Psycho* vibe. The only thing missing was a Kostabi painting. Her room was also a warehouse of sex toys, lovingly displayed on chrome shelves like tchotchkes in a grandma's curio cabinet. There were speculums, dildos, hospital equipment and carefully arranged stacks of porn. At the center of the room sat a king-sized bed and on the bed, a fluffy cat named Spike. Annie offered me a glass of water and showed me her collection of schoolgirl outfits. Handing me a gray one, she told me to put it on.

She told me that the client we were about to see insisted on being referred to as "Lord H."

"He's my heaviest client," she added. "But because you're new, he'll go easy on you."

I asked her if she used her dungeon name "Penelope" now that she worked from home.

"Nah…it gets too confusing. They're paying my rent so I don't really care if they know my real name."

Lord H had provided Annie with her schoolgirl outfit collection, which he had purchased during excursions abroad, trips paid for by his employer, the church. Lord H was a priest. According to Annie, he was practically employee of the month and so popular with the church that he was on the brink of being promoted to bishop.

*Holy Christ,* I thought. Either Annie was insane and making this up, or I was about to do something considered *very bad* by the general populace. All those little old ladies who filled the collection plate at church every week hoping to get into heaven—this is where their dollars went. Had I any belief in heaven or hell, I would've walked out of the room instantly.

Even though he wasn't a bishop *yet*, I began to think of Lord H as *the Bishop*.

Lord H arrived. He was tall, big-boned, distinguished and almost handsome. He wore a dark suit, had a grey beard and salt-and-pepper hair. His eyebrows stuck up in points at the center, which made him look vaguely satanic. He smiled gaily as he entered the room.

"Lord H, this is June," Annie said casually.

"Nice to meet you," he said, kissing my hand.

Annie had already changed into a gray schoolgirl outfit that matched my own, which seemed to smash her C-cup breasts down to an A-cup. Lord H sat down at the edge of Annie's bed and Spike jumped off fearfully.

"Annie, why don't we warm you up?" he suggested. Annie waltzed over to him and lay across his lap on her stomach. He lifted his hand in the air and brought it all the way down with a thud. I flinched just watching him spank her. I'd never seen a person get spanked so hard. It was inhumane.

Roughly, he pulled her uniform up and her panties down, continuing his assault on her bottom, which grew redder than a baboon's ass in heat by the time he let her go. She got up, looking dazed. Rubbing both cheeks frantically, she examined them in the mirror.

"Your turn, June," he said.

Were there a hell, I was now about to secure my place in it. Maybe I was already there.

Lying down on my stomach, I closed my eyes and breathed. His hand came down with such force I cried out. He ignored me, yanked my panties down and kept going, never slowing his pace. Sweat covered my forehead and my eyes watered. This went on for probably five minutes though it felt like eternity.

"Okay, I think you've had enough," he finally said, letting me go.

"She's being very good," Annie remarked as I stood in front of Lord H, pulling my panties back up.

He then stood up and began caressing me over my uniform. He leaned down and kissed me on the lips as though I were his lover, an act that made me more uncomfortable than shoving a dildo up a stranger's ass.

"Lie down on your back," he said to me, motioning toward the bed. I lay on my back. "Now you get on top of her," he said to Annie.

Annie climbed over me, pulled my panties off and began to lick my pussy. I imagined what we were doing must be illegal. Or was it? If he paid us to perform oral sex on him, that would be illegal but what we did *in front of him* was our business. Plus we were at Annie's place, far away from the long arm of the law. The dungeons were constantly getting busted and that's why most of the girls were on guard. (That and the fact that some of them actually considered prostitution demeaning and/or morally wrong!) But in Annie's emporium of perversion we were safe. We were all on the same page, one in which getting what we needed—be it money or sadistic pleasure—outweighed any notions of morality.

Annie was a pussy-eating expert—not that there is a *right way* to eat a pussy, but there *is* a *wrong way*. To ignore the clit and to not be passionate about it are the two biggest mistakes one can make, but Annie made neither. As she fucked me with her tongue, I looked over her shoulder at H who was rubbing Annie's cunt with his fingers.

"Let's have some fun," he suddenly said as if he weren't already having fun. "Have you ever had a whole fist in your pussy, June?" he asked.

"No, Sir."

"Do you think Annie could fit her fist in your pussy?" he asked.

"I don't know." I really had no idea, but I was about to find out.

I lay on my back, frightened while Annie produced a tube of K-Y. She warmed a generous amount between her hands and lay beside me. She inserted two fingers in my pussy, followed slowly by a third.

*There is no way this is going to work,* I thought, as my pussy stretched to what I imagined was its limit. Soon though, her pinky was inside of me whereupon Lord H whipped out a Polaroid camera and snapped a close-up of my stretched-out vertical smile.

After working her first four fingers in, her thumb joined the crowd and I began to sweat profusely. Squirming around, I hoped she would remove her fist at the sight of my agonized face. Lord H took one last Polaroid and then assured Annie that she could remove her fist.

"Now it's your turn," Lord H said to Annie, and I reciprocated the fisting while Annie squirmed.

Following the fisting fiasco, Lord H instructed Annie and me to bend over the bed and stick our bottoms in the air. He picked up a flogger and beat us mercilessly. Floggers usually aren't too painful, but the way he used them made me long for a caning.

"You've got a great ass," he said, hoisting my skirt over my waist. He then spanked me with his bare hand and moved his fingers between my legs, roughly inserting them into my cunt.

"Get on your knees," he demanded, standing up and undoing his pants. Assuming he wanted me to get on my knees in order to suck him off, I took him in my mouth while Annie watched. This, I knew, was illegal. Oddly enough, I didn't care. His penis was not very large, but it swelled between my lips. As I continued to suck and lick, Annie stood behind me while Lord H reached around and spanked her.

"You're doing a good job," Annie assured me when Lord H abruptly pulled out of my mouth and sat back down on the bed. He reached for a wooden hairbrush and motioned for me to bend over his lap. He pushed my head toward his cock so I continued to suck on him. He then took the hairbrush and began to spank me with it. It was the most painful implement of torture my ass had ever come into contact with.

Screaming, I tried to wiggle out of his arms, but he held me down and pushed my head toward his wilting penis.

"Please stop," I begged and he finally let me go. Now it was Annie's turn. She took the hairbrush better than me but she still squirmed and cried. Rubbing my ass, I could see in the mirror that it was now purple and red.

Finally, Annie slid off his lap as I had done.

"June, why don't you show Annie some pleasure?" he suggested. Stretching out over Annie I licked her dripping pussy as she had done for me. Meanwhile Lord H began to insert a finger in my ass.

"How would you like to let me fuck you in the ass?" he whispered to me.

*What doesn't kill you only makes you stronger*, I thought, but my asshole didn't agree. It tightened up in fear around his finger.

Ignoring my spastic asshole, I said, "OK." The fact that I said this still shocks me. Not only was this prostitution, it was anal and it was with a member of the church. I hate anal sex, but I think I hate the church even more. And, despite the fact that my previous sessions had physically turned me on, I was, in this instance, far from aroused possibly because Lord H's personality was so repugnant. Annie slid out from under me and lay at my side. Lord H grabbed her ass and fondled it, spanking it lightly. He then got up to fetch a condom.

"Is this okay with you?" Annie whispered.

"Yes."

Lord H rolled the condom onto his penis, which still wilted a bit. Annie remedied this by sucking on it for a few seconds. He then slicked it up with K-Y and attempted to guide it into my asshole with his hand. It took a few tries before he was able to insert it. Once it was in, he drove it in hard. Annie grabbed my hands and squeezed them maternally as tears rolled down my cheeks. Trying to relax, I breathed in and out, but when Lord H began beating me with the hairbrush while he fucked me up the ass, I felt that I might lose consciousness.

*Be somewhere else,* I told myself. I imagined that I was asleep and this was a nightmare.

"Will you take the hairbrush for me like a good girl?" he whispered into my ear.

"Yes."

"Will you bleed for me?"

"Yes, Sir."

This pushed him over the edge and he came.

He lay on top of me until I told him I had to pee and he let me go.

Once up, I hastily changed into my street clothes and got ready to leave. I felt deliriously impatient, like someone who'd been in prison for twenty years and was about to walk free. Annie kissed me on the cheek and Lord H handed me an envelope full of cash, which alleviated the pain in my ass greatly. We made tentative plans to "do it again" soon.

When I left the Chelsea Hotel, it was close to 7 p.m. Stripe Shirts were just getting off work, sitting at outdoor cafés, enjoying drinks with other Stripe Shirts. Much as they could probably never imagine letting a priest ass-fuck them for cash, I could never imagine being in their shoes, going to an office day after day.

I suppose I should have felt more like a failure given I was now officially a prostitute, but I didn't. I'm not saying I felt like a winner either. I guess I didn't feel much of anything and coincidentally, this made me feel very much like a prostitute.

## Chapter 7

## *Hi Lo*

"Up the ASS?!! And for five hundred dollars?!! Holy shit! That guy got the bargain of his life!" Tommy declared. He said this loudly enough that everyone in Barramundi's garden stared in horror.

Tommy Read was a master of inappropriate behavior—a good drinking buddy of Kyle's who'd, in recent years, become my good drinking buddy. We talked almost every day and I'd harbored a secret crush on him for months. He was in his late twenties, an Ivy League educated, smart-assed cynic who quit his job on Wall Street to become a freelance writer and comedian. He was effortlessly stylish and cute with longish sandy blonde hair and big brown eyes. He wore perfectly tailored blazers (which he never had laundered) always over the same worn-out black t-shirt he loved so much he had it professionally laundered weekly.

"It's my lucky black t-shirt," he'd say. "I'm not taking any chances on it." The people at the Laundromat laughed at him.

Whereas Kyle and Stuart seemed to think of me as too fragile for the sex industry, Tommy realized I had a toughness that belied my innocent appearance. He once said to me, "Dylan told me you can take the heaviest session of any submissive she knows. What's really weird is, when she said this, I felt kind of proud of you."

I'd met up with Tommy and Kyle at the bar after leaving the Chelsea. It was one of those warm spring nights where suddenly *everyone* in New York City is out, all ready to get crazy like dormice who've just emerged from hibernation. Even though I wasn't exactly in the mood for fun (or even for sitting down) it's almost a crime against nature to stay home on nights like this. Plus, I figured a few pints might act as an anesthetic.

Kyle needed an anesthetic for his heart since Jessicunt had been living up to her name. Just as he really started to fall for her, she grew cold, started blowing him off and treating his apartment like a Manhattan Mini Storage. She'd leave her stuff there and come over at 4 a.m. after getting off work at her bartending job. Usually she was wasted and she'd pass out and not have sex with him, not even the next morning after he'd cooked her breakfast. Tommy, on the other hand, was eternally single, having sabotaged every date he'd been on in the past six months. We were the perfect company for each other, all of us mildly depressed. There's nothing worse than being dejected and surrounded by high-energy, joyous people. In fact, a recent study indicated that New Yorkers are less likely to kill themselves because everyone in New York is depressed. Whereas if you are in Utah or somewhere and you're depressed and everyone around you is happy and gay, you'll be a lot more likely to swallow a handful of pills.

The other great thing about Kyle and Tommy is that I

could tell them anything, every hideous detail of my session with the bishop and neither of them judged me. Tommy seemed to think my worst sin was not asking for an extra five hundred when it came to anal sex.

"Where's Stu been?" Kyle asked, probably because he saw me staring at the door, hoping Stu would walk through it.

"I don't know. The last time I saw him was a week ago. We walked over the Brooklyn Bridge at three in the morning then went back to my place and he fucked me so hard we broke my box spring. He's not calling so he's obviously either fucking other people or taking some new drug I don't know about. And now I'm sleeping on a broken box spring with a sore ass."

"Alice, what you need to do is immediately bone someone else," Tommy suggested. "It'll make you feel better."

"Or it'll make me feel worse."

Kyle agreed, "If the sex is bad it makes it a lot worse."

"There's no harm in trying," Tommy said, smiling in a way that made me think he was suggesting I bone him.

"I can't imagine having sex with anyone here," Kyle said looking around.

"Me neither," I agreed. It was nothing but Stripe Shirts and people who looked like they'd been drinking every day since the Dutch settled Manhattan. Tommy was the only person I liked and I liked him so much, I worried sleeping with him would ruin everything.

"You two need to cheer the fuck up," Tommy said. "I took the subway uptown today to pick up my check. There was a homeless man on the train and he kept taking his shoe off and smelling it. He asked me for the time. I said, 'It's a quarter of eleven.' We sat there in silence and after a while he said, 'Have a nice day!' He was the happiest person on the subway."

"Are you saying we should become homeless?" I asked.

"No, but maybe happiness isn't that complicated. All these dudes at the dungeon you tell me about. Look at the lengths they go to in order to *try* to be happy and they're miserable—more miserable than you and you're the one being tortured. I'm just saying *happiness* is a state of mind. A delusional state of mind."

"Yeah," Kyle agreed. "It's reserved for people who are on drugs, children and dogs."

"People who are on drugs are only happy when they have the drugs," I countered. I've often said I fear happiness the way crackheads fear running out of crack. Happiness never lasts. "Then again, people who say they are high on life are full of shit. I have been 'on life' for twenty-three years and I'm still waiting for the high to kick in. It just doesn't work as well as booze, cigs or even coffee. Happiness is only available in minute doses."

"I don't know. I feel pretty happy most of the time," Kyle said, "but I want happiness and stability and all I've got is happiness and chaos. The chaos makes it hard to even notice the happiness."

"But do you think people who have stability are happy?" Tommy asked. "They're so busy maintaining stability they don't have time for highs and lows."

"I just wish the highs and lows could be a little less high and low," I said.

"Do you know that game on the *Price is Right* called Hi Lo?" Kyle asked. "It's the one where you get six items and three of them go in the 'high-priced aisle' and three of them go in the 'low-priced' aisle and if you mess up Bob sends you home with a shit parting gift and you never get to be in the Showcase Showdown."

"Yeah. I know that game. Not as good as the Alpine Climber," Tommy said.

"Of course not, but it's way more stressful because there's no room for error. Hi Lo is like a metaphor for life. Happy. Sad. Everyone's main emotion is fear, terror at making the wrong choices and being sent home," Kyle said.

"Are you stoned?" Tommy asked.

"A little."

The garden closed at midnight. Otherwise, angry neighbors threw eggs on the crowd. So we moved our philosophical *Price is Right* dialogue inside where Lucille poured us shots of something sweet and strong and we toasted to dogs and children and Bob Barker. Kyle eventually declared exhaustion and went home to "masturbate to gay porn" while Tommy and I stuck around for more drinks and more talk. We both agreed that "good talk" was one of the most important things in life, right after food and shelter. It was why he'd sabotaged date after date, his inability to deal with the endless stream of dull questions they asked—*What do you do? What does your dad do? Where'd you go to school?* Like reciting your résumé instead of having fun.

We talked and drank ourselves silly and he walked me home afterward since the neighborhood was still a dangerous shit-hole in those days. Despite the recent influx of Stripe Shirts, crack paraphernalia and heroin were then readily available in bodegas that sold one dusty can of coke and one package of Twizzlers, likely manufactured around the same time as the earth's crust. My first month in my Ludlow Street apartment, I'd woken up to the sound of gunshots several times and once dealt with a lunatic who broke into our building. He was chased away by a knife-wielding Dominican neighbor before making the unwise decision to dive out the fourth floor's hallway window into a narrow alley unreachable from the street. EMT workers had to throw a pulley from my window over to the roof of the abandoned building next door then into the alley to get the would-be cat burglar who probably broke both legs in the process. I lent the cops all of my blankets to bundle the man up, which they promised to wash and return (but never did.)

More recently, a woman had been raped in my building's hallway before being dragged to an ATM and robbed at gunpoint so not even the massive canister of pepper spray, which served as my keychain made me feel safe. Both Kyle and Tommy always made a point of, not just walking me home, but walking me *inside* my building and halfway up the stairs.

When we got to the third floor, we stopped to say goodbye. Tommy looked me in the eyes. "Listen to me," he said, "This is the most clichéd bullshit on the planet, but I've gotta say it– *It's always darkest before the dawn.*"

"Well dawn better hurry the fuck up."

"It never does, Alice. You just gotta wait and you gotta work hard."

"I know. I need to lay off the sauce and actually write something."

"Me too. Sometimes I watch the Oscars and I think that should be me up there winning best screenplay and then I remember I've never written a screenplay. But we'll get there."

"I hope so."

"Think of this as your 'Howard Roark working in the quarry' phase. You're just busting your ass out there. Meanwhile, I'm in my MICKEY Rourke phase."

"Which Mickey Rourke?"

"I'm thinking *Diner* with a touch of *Wild Orchid*."

"That is the worst possible influence I could ever imagine. I should definitely go inside."

"Come here first," he said, reaching out to give me a hug. Wrapping my arms around him, I hung on, limp and tired, my body aching like I'd been beaten probably because I had. For the second time that day, I felt the tears come.

"Goodbye," I said and climbed the final three flights, trying like the little *Price is Right* alpine climber not to fall. Once inside, I plopped into bed, closed my eyes and waited for the dawn.

# Chapter 8
## The Lynns of the World

Compared to my hour with Lord H, most sessions at The Inferno were pretty run-of-the-mill. I can't begin to tell you how popular spanking is. Parents—don't spank your kids unless you want them to spend thousands of dollars sexualizing it later in life.

Sometimes role-play was thrown in, which livened up the spanking, paddling and bondage. I did a session in The Inferno's "classroom" with a big, southern man named Ken who was visiting New York on business. He wanted me to portray "Lynn," a schoolgirl being punished for smoking. Seeing as how I was always trying to quit smoking, this seemed like the perfect opportunity for behavioral therapy. He would play the school's principal who found a pack of smokes and an ashtray in my locker. A teen caring enough about tidiness to squirrel away an ashtray already seemed ridiculous, but I went with it. Ken, the principal, knew that I was a "good girl" and that I was just experimenting. Still, he had no choice but to punish me with a spanking, either that, or call my parents. Within Ken's fantasy, my parents were odious sadists. Calling them would produce a punishment so horrifying I would have no choice but to accept the spanking. What's funny is that in "real life" my parents never punished me at all. I was the youngest of six and they'd given up on discipline by the time I was born.

Principal Ken reached for an invisible phone as I teetered around in front of him on my high-heeled Mary Janes. I loved the fact that miming was involved. It was almost like one of my one-person shows. No money for props.

"Please, no, Sir. Anything but that! I'll be grounded, and they'll beat me far worse than you will. I'll take the spanking!" I said.

"Okay, but this is *our* secret. No one's going to find out about this. If anyone at school hears about this, I'll call your parents."

"Yes, Sir."

"Lynn," he said, motioning to a leather paddle and a wooden paddle, "I'm going to use these on your bottom. Spread your legs and bend over the table. You're going to get twenty, and I want you to count."

Once my paddling was complete, he led me to a suspension bar where I was still Lynn but he was suddenly a perverted exercise instructor trying to convince me that the suspension bar was really a piece of exercise equipment. Lynn, he explained, was an aspiring dancer keen on getting into shape. (Side note—he'd requested Lynn wear a black bra under a white shirt so she was also a "Glamour Don't.")

He fastened my wrists to the suspension bar's cuffs then cranked it up until I was on my tiptoes.

"All the dancers use this, Lynn," he said, letting his hands graze between my thighs. "Are you gonna be a good girl and let me touch your pussy? Are you gonna do everything I ask?"

"Yes, Sir."

He pulled my panties aside and worked two fingers inside my pussy, moving them in and out.

"You know all the boys can see your black bra under your white shirt?"

"I didn't know that, Sir."

"I'll let you down but only if you're a very good girl, only if you'll let me watch you play with yourself."

"Yes, Sir. I'll do anything for you."

He stopped suddenly, snapped out of character and said, "You *became* her right there. That was amazing."

So somewhere out there a "Lynn" existed. I hoped she was very far back in his past. I also hoped to Christ he wasn't actually a gym teacher or principal.

He freed me from suspension and led me to the leather table where I lay down and spread my legs. He undid his trousers and removed his underwear.

"Do you see what you've done to me?" he asked, pointing to his fully erect cock. "Are you proud of this?"

He then began to stroke himself while I mutually masturbated or at least, pretended to. The arousal I'd felt in my first sessions had begun to fade, replaced by an ennui with everything that was happening. My pussy was now so dry, I may has well have been working at the Taco Bell Drive-Thru.

So many sessions transpired like the one with Ken, where we were in a Land of Make Believe where the Dom was getting revenge against someone who'd hurt or rejected him in the past. Money was the great democratizer, the thing that made the Lynns of the world horny for men like Ken.

## Chapter 9

## *Mrs. Thompson*

My session with Ken was immediately followed by a session with "Ivan." He asked that I dress in secretarial gear, which was not something I kept in my dungeon locker or even in my closet at home. I borrowed a suit from Dylan as well as her heels, which were at least two sizes too big for me. I knotted my hair back and wore a black push up bra and g-string (as per his request.)

I shuffled back to the door of the fake classroom, feeling a lot like I was playing dress-up. Ivan opened the door a crack and eyed me suspiciously before letting me in. He was at least a foot taller than me, a skinny man with a pointed nose and graying brown hair.

"Hi June," he said in a monotone.

"Hi."

"I brought some extra things. I was hoping you could put them on."

He handed me a bag containing a pair of black, lace-trimmed thigh highs, a pair of taupe nylons and a pair of cream-colored nylon granny panties.

"I want you to put the thigh-highs on first, then the nylons and then on top of the nylons, wear the panties." He explained. Despite the fact that this was a felony of a fashion faux pas, I did as told.

Ivan wanted me to play "Mrs. Thompson" a high-school teacher while he played "Tom", a senior in high school. Tom was a delinquent who was always late for class. And in the particular scenario Ivan wanted us to enact, Mrs. Thompson would be tired. After a long day of teaching, she just wanted to clean the chalkboard and go home. Yet despite her tiredness, she would feel horny, so horny that as she erases the chalkboard, she sways her hips back and forth seductively. Then, she would grow so overwhelmed that she would begin to masturbate, thrusting her crotch against the side of the desk.

And this is when Tom would enter the room and catch her!

"You try to pretend like you weren't up to anything naughty, but I know better," Ivan explained. "You try to bring up my horrible grades and my attendance problems, but I don't let you change the subject. I then corner you and make you confess your secret crush on me at which point I begin to order you around. You completely lose your authority."

Ivan sat at the other end of the classroom as I began to enact the horny teacher scenario, which I found incredibly embarrassing especially since my outfit was so heinous. Someone from a previous session had written, "I will not be a slut" repeatedly on the chalkboard. As I began to erase it, I swayed my hips back and forth, finally masturbating over my clothes. I then thrust my crotch into the corner of the desk as instructed.

That's when Ivan entered and I turned around with a shocked expression on my face.

"Tom! What are you doing here?"

"I came to talk to you about after-school activities."

"Now really isn't a good time, Tom. I was just getting ready to go home."

"I can see that."

We went back and forth with dialogue so cheesy it belonged in '70s porn. Ivan, who had become the unruly delinquent, Tom, reached his hand out and caressed my chest. He undid the top button on my white blouse.

"Tom, this has gone way too far."

"Oh come on. Your husband probably can't even get it up anymore. Everyone knows what's on your mind. You can look at it if you want," he added, undoing his zipper in order to show me the bulge in his briefs.

He ran his hand between my thighs and rubbed my crotch, which was still buried under several layers of clothing.

"Tell me you need it," he said.

"I need it."

"What do you need?"

"I need cock."

"Good girl. Take off your jacket and top."

I unbuttoned my blouse and let my suit jacket fall. Ivan then pushed my bra aside and grabbed my breasts. He told me to turn around and bend over the desk. Doing so, he began to spank me.

"Are you gonna do everything I say?" he asked.

"Yes, Sir."

The spanking subsided after a few minutes and I then felt a heavy flogger on my ass and upper back.

"I've really enjoyed your class Mrs. Thompson," he teased while flogging me, and I wondered if there had been a real Mrs. Thompson in his childhood. Maybe he sat through high school awkwardly attempting to disguise a boner with his books then ran home each day to jack off to a variety of Mrs. Thompson fantasies. Strange that I'd just played a schoolgirl dealing with a principal and I was now a teacher dealing with a schoolboy.

"Stand up," he said, dropping his pants and pulling off his briefs.

I stood up and faced him, and he began to kiss my neck, biting into the flesh.

"Take off your skirt now."

Wobbling on the too-big pumps, I peeled the skirt off to reveal the granny panties.

"Good. Now, I want you to walk over to the suspension bar."

He fastened me into the suspension bar and cranked it up before spanking me and spinning me around lightly.

He moved his hands between my thighs and rubbed the cotton crotch of the granny panties, pulling them down roughly.

"Are you ready to be a slut for me?" he asked.

"Yes, Sir."

He then dug his nails into the taupe stockings forming a giant run down the thigh. He continued to tear at the stockings until they hung in tatters from my legs. After which, he let me down from the suspension bar.

I stood in the center of the room, now clad in the lace

thigh-highs, the tattered stockings, black g-string and push-up bra.

"Take your hair down and shake it out," he said.

I unpinned my hair and shook it out like a librarian gone wild.

"Take off your shoes. Remove the torn stockings and then place your shoes on the floor in front of you."

I did as told, happy to be rid of the heels.

"Now, get down on your knees and kiss your shoes."

The cold floor hurt my knees as I bent down to kiss the pumps.

"Good girl. Now stand up and put the shoes back on."

I did as told, slipping the shoes back onto my feet.

"Good. Now slowly walk back and forth in front of me."

"You look like a real slut now," he commented. (Funny, because I felt like one too.) "Now, take off one shoe and place it in front of you."

I removed one shoe and placed it in front of me, heel down. He then turned it over so the spiked heel faced upward.

"Now, I want you to grind your pussy onto that shoe."

The task of squatting over the shoe while wearing only one high heel, which was too big to begin with, was difficult to say the least. With the precision of a ninja, I lowered myself onto it, sweeping my pussy over the heel.

"I want you to fuck the heel," he said and I obeyed, feeling guilty for violating Dylan's expensive shoes.

"Fuck that shoe," he cheered. "Fuck it like the little slut you are."

He groaned with pleasure as he sat back in one of the rickety, wooden chairs and began to stroke his cock.

Sensing that he was ready to come, I lifted the shoe up and fucked myself with it. If he wanted me to act like a little slut, I was happy to do so if it meant chopping ten minutes off my session.

"Do it harder!" he moaned, jacking himself silly until he finally came.

Once he'd settled down and cleaned up, he quickly transformed from Tom back into Ivan. I pulled my suit back on and transformed from Mrs. Thompson back into June who would later transform back into Alice. I felt like Sybil, I'd been so many people in one day. Plus, I'd fucked a shoe. It hadn't even been my own shoe. Would I ever have a normal sex life again?

# Chapter 10

## *Three Choices*

Not long after my session at the Chelsea, Annie called and proposed we do another session together, this time with a Japanese businessman named William. Annie had seen him many times, and told me it would pay three hundred dollars for an easy hour. She said he had "unusual" fetishes, but there would be no sex, and we could amuse each other in the midst of our torment.

For this session, she'd rented out a room at dungeon called Avalon. Sadly, there was nothing magical or elfin about Avalon. It was a lot like a less lavish version of The Inferno, actually.

William began the session by asking us to strip naked, which we did. He then asked us to put on thick, black, leather collars he'd brought with him. My collar was so massive that it looked like I was being treated for whiplash.

He then stripped naked and I was shocked to find that, despite his frail appearance, he was sporting one of the largest erections I'd ever seen.

He told Annie and me to face each other, and put our hands behind our heads. Taking out a pair of nipple clamps, he attached one clamp to my right nipple and the other to Annie's left nipple so that a chain attached us. Annie barely flinched. I, on the other hand, had to do Lamaze breathing in order to deal with the pain. My nipples are so small that most clamps cover them entirely. He pulled on the chain and jiggled it around.

*Don't think about it. Don't think about it. It'll all be over soon,* I repeated in my head. As if to silence my thoughts, he ball-gagged me and told me to snap my fingers if it grew too painful. I had come to realize I didn't mind ball-gags because they kept me from having to say anything cheesy or insincere. In "real life" I can't seem to shut up, but in sessions, I wanted nothing more than to be quiet. He then slipped a blindfold over my eyes, but it was flimsy and let a lot of light in, so that I could cheat if need be.

Once I was blindfolded, his body, cock included, pressed up against my back while he caressed my aching right breast. He then removed the blindfold, gag and nipple clamp.

He led Annie and me to the doorway, which led to the "library," which was filled with whips and chains and books that no one ever read, along with a desk that no one ever sat at unless maybe they were tied to it. He put wrist and ankle cuffs on Annie and attached her wrists to eyehooks at the top of the doorway. Her ankles, he attached to hooks at the bottom of the doorway.

"This is my favorite position," Annie giggled.

Producing two wooden clothespins, he attached them to the skin just above her armpits. He then took two plastic clothespins with little silver weights on the ends of them, and attached them to her labia. While this sounds painful, it's not. However, any type of clamp, clip or weight on the clit is excruciating.

Annie looked down at the weights and said, "So, this is what it's like to have balls."

He then took out a set of nipple clamps and attached them to her nipples.

"Okay," he said, turning to me, "Now we are going to play a game. I'm going to blindfold you, and you are going to remove these with your mouth." He gestured to the clothespins, "Start here and work your way down."

He slipped the blindfold over my eyes. Moving my tongue gently across her body, I found the first clothespin. It reminded me of the game "Operation" and I thought about how greed is the central theme of all games. A friend of mine once pointed out that most children's games can be summed up as, "You get all your things, you put 'em in your thing, and then you win!"

And S&M is like a board game with human game pieces. I removed each clamp and clip deftly. If this were an Olympic event, I'd be a gold medalist. She breathed a sigh of relief each time I removed another piece. When I got down to the final pieces, I let my tongue linger before removing them. I handed him the final piece with my mouth.

"Get down on your knees, and kiss her," he instructed. Since she was standing, I assumed he meant for me to kiss her on the *vagina*.

After I had properly shown her some affection, he suggested we reverse the game. This time he tied me up, and let Annie go to work. Although it was pretty painful, it was less work than removing the clips.

Annie removed the clothespins with ease, but when she

got to the nipple clamps, I got panicky because they wouldn't come off. Horrific, Goya-like visions of my chest being separated from my body entered my mind but they were for naught because after a bit of tugging the clamps came off.

Stripped of my ornaments, William suggested we worship his feet. He had remarkably clean feet, and I was happy to endure a physically painless activity for a change. Of course, the foot worship lasted only a moment before he conjured up another challenge. William seemed to have sexual ADD.

"How well do you girls know each other?" he asked.

"Do you know what Annie's into?" he asked me, and I thought, *Yeah, making money and getting the fuck out of this business.*

Instead I told him I thought I knew Annie fairly well. Truth was, I hardly knew Annie at all.

He continued, "I'm going to give Annie three choices. She'll tell me which activity she prefers. You will then have to guess which activity she chose. If you guess wrong, you will have to perform or endure that activity. If you guess right, she will."

Annie's three choices were: A.) Have her feet whipped twenty times. B.) Suck William's cock or, C.) Shove the end of a bullwhip up her ass.

Given this predicament, I instinctively chose the one that *I* would mind the least. If I guessed wrong, I would be saving Annie from torment, and if I guessed right I would save myself. I knew Annie hated foot torture, but it never bothered my calloused, pedestrian feet. Not to mention, it seemed infinitely less messy and time consuming than a blowjob, and as for the bullwhip up the ass, I have never been comfortable shoving anything other than dildos, Q-tips, penises or tampons into my body. So I chose A.

I was flabbergasted when Annie revealed that she'd chosen C.

So, I got to play the martyr, and have my feet whipped while Annie laughed at me the whole time. But the whipping *was* completely painless *and* I got to lie down. After my punishment we reversed the game. My choices were the following: A.) Wear a pair of nipple clamps and remove them with my teeth. B.) Have my pussy whipped twenty times, or C.) Shove a lit candle up my ass. (Not the lit end, obviously.)

The nipple clamps were out. My nipples still ached from the session's previous nipple torture, and the candle was out for reasons I've already covered. The obvious winner was B.

I'm certain Annie knew this but rather than guess wrong and play the martyr, she guessed correctly. While B was my choice, it was not going to be fun. My pussy, unlike my calloused feet, is delicate. Beads of sweat ran slowly down my back as they tied me up.

I lay down on the leather bed at the center of the room. They bound my hands over my head and tied my legs spread eagle, so as to make my pussy an easier target. In a lecherous move, William combined A and B, and made me wear nipple clamps while receiving the whipping.

After my whipping, William asked Annie, "Is she ticklish? Do you want to tickle her?"

"Yes, Master," she said.

William untied my legs and then, with rope, tied my ankles to the chain that connected my nipple clamps to each other. They both began to tickle me and my first impulse was to thrash around, but I quickly realized that each movement sent shockwaves of pain through my nipples. I therefore remained perfectly still until after a few minutes, they got bored and untied me.

William had mentioned earlier that he wanted us to dominate him at the end of the session so Annie suggested we switch roles. I don't really like being dominant. When I'm passive it feels natural, but when I'm dominant it feels like an act. Maybe I'm a romantic, but I feel that there needs to be some love in the equation. The most authentic games occur between loved ones. The only men who ever really knew how to torture me were the ones I loved and the only men I've tortured properly were the ones who loved me.

Annie took control of the situation and suggested I get William a collar. I brought him a black leather collar and fastened it around his neck. He looked pathetic. Annie told him he was a good slave and ordered him to kneel before us and kiss our feet. I worried maybe my feet were dirty. If they were, he obviously didn't mind. I picked up a paddle and nonchalantly paddled his rear while Annie twisted his nipples. Finally, she told him to lie down.

"You're a good slave," we cooed together because having just been slaves, we knew how important appreciation was. I thrust my foot in and out of his mouth as Annie verbally tormented him.

"Maybe we should use you as our personal toilet and pee all over you. I bet you'd like that you little slut! Maybe if you're not good, we'll drag you out into the hallway on a leash and have all the other Mistresses make fun of you!"

She opened the door to the hallway in order to make her threat more real. A look of total ecstasy came over him as his hands furiously groped at his cock. Annie and I encouraged him, and he began to stroke his penis while we played with his nipples. Since Annie had seen William before, she knew what to do, brutally twisting his nipples.

"Harder," he moaned and we twisted crazily until at long last, he came. A look of relief and joy spread across his face, a look that was soon replaced with a sheepish expression that so many clients wore at session's end. I felt sorry for them, going about their seemingly normal lives while obsessing over nipple clamps, gags, clothespins, collars, feet and everything else.

William seemed like a nice guy and he was one client who later opened up to me, not because I pried but because he desperately *wanted* to open up. I once asked him if he ever suggested anything kinky to his wife.

"You don't get it," he said, "We are old-fashioned. She thinks blowjobs are kinky. You have no idea how lucky you are to be so free."

I hadn't been at the dungeon long, but I was starting to realize he was right. Even though I was a slave, I was freer than most.

## Chapter 11

## *The Catsuit*

Never at any point, did the bishop wear a sheepish expression. Despite the hypocrisy of his actions, he never looked guilty or conflicted. I'm pretty sure he had convinced himself that his subs *loved* getting beaten black and blue. Either that or he felt the entire human race owed him total submission.

Despite Tommy, Will and even Dylan's suggestion that I don't "go there" again, I started doing monthly sessions with Annie and the bishop. There were sometimes variations to the hour but they always ended the same way—him fucking me while he beat me with the hairbrush and asked me if I'd bleed for him.

I always said yes and this always made him come.

"The problem with the whole 'what doesn't kill you only makes you stronger' adage, is that this lunatic bishop or priest or whatever the fuck he is could kill you. And the bastard would get away with it," Kyle said.

"He's a sadist, Kyle, not a murderer."

"Well, he's a sick fuck."

I hadn't mentioned the sick fuck to Stu who'd recently made a brief appearance in my apartment, staggering in with a 6-pack of Bud, so drunk he could hardly stand. I was lonely for warm caresses, lonely for conversation and aching physically. He'd promised me a massage but simply "stuck it in" about two minutes into rubbing my back. I wasn't entirely disappointed. After so many wilting cocks at the dungeon, it was nice to get a good hard fucking, in a bed, without whips and chains, even if the person fucking me couldn't tell if it were night or day.

Now Stu was on tour in the Midwest and I was trying to put a little of the energy I'd spent obsessing over him into painting and writing. I started writing erotica, some of it based on my dungeon experiences. But I felt a bit like de Sade writing in prison, convinced my essays would never see the light of day. Meanwhile, my paintings had become more innocent. They were a lot like Victorian Fairy paintings, all rainbows, fawns, castles and mushrooms—magical universes far from the clutches of The Inferno, the Chelsea and Avalon where I'd begun to see more clients with Annie. The Chelsea was great for guys like the bishop who didn't need a lot of props, but for some clients, leather beds, suspension bars and wooden horses were required. Avalon had all that and more.

Jeremy was one such client. He used to see Annie at The Inferno, but when she quit he started seeing me. When I told him we were now doing private sessions together, he was overjoyed.

He was into "sensual domination"—a lot of flogging and caressing but *not a lot of pain.* At The Inferno, our sessions had gotten sexual, but the furthest I'd gone was jacking him off. Even so, I knew something after my first session with the bishop—now that I'd had sex with one person for money, I would do it again. This is why it's often described as a "descent" into prostitution. You fall fast because you've got nothing to lose. I quickly mastered the art of saying *fuck it*.

So if Jeremy wanted to fuck me, I was fine with it. But I would only fuck him outside of The Inferno. I kind of liked Richard and Clarissa, but there was no way either would reap one cent off of my vagina even if occasionally, I liked fucking for money. And it turns out I really liked fucking Jeremy. The money just made it better. And dirtier. The taboo against prostitution is sometimes a turn-on for both parties. Everyone says men pay prostitutes to *leave,* but I think men pay prostitutes *to be prostitutes.*

Jeremy enjoyed theatrics and he often brought Annie and me costumes, which were usually destroyed by session's end.

My favorite of these was *the catsuit.*

He blushed as he handed me the package.

"I'm sorry. I know it's tasteless, but it's rippable. That's the important thing," he apologized.

"Don't worry," I said. "I love trashy things."

Opening the package, I gasped. It was a *Josie and the Pussycat*s style, leopard-print catsuit.

"This is beautiful." I gushed. As a child I'd worshipped Josie and the Pussycats—those wiry ladies in catsuits, congregating with the ultimate fashion icon—their evil manager– Alexander Cabot the Third. With his bowl haircut and groovy glasses, Alexander was the first cartoon beatnik and my first crush.

Slipping into the skin-tight leotard, I felt like a superheroine.

"Oh my god, you look amazing. That actually looks good on you," he said.

He then explained the following scenario— Annie would blindfold me and place cuffs on my wrists and ankles. She would then drag me into the room on a leash and present me, as a gift to him. She would play the experienced slave and I would play the naïve pupil. It was a routine we'd perfected.

Annie ordered me to kneel. Doing so, I looked up at her curvaceous body and thought, *I am jealous of the entire world of shapely blondes, yet I am also attracted to them.* The first woman I ever had a crush on was named Dawn. She was about fifteen and I was about twelve. I saw her for the first time at the roller-rink. She had shoulder-length blonde feathered hair and wore light blue eye shadow, dark Gloria Vanderbilt jeans and white roller-skates with lavender pompoms. She drank and smoked and probably wasn't a virgin. I was under the impression that she ruled the universe. I often wonder what Dawn is doing today and I imagine she's probably graduated to doing Meth.

Annie brings out the same impulse that Dawn did years ago. I want to bask in her delinquency and aggressive sexuality. As I stared at Annie's black-lace bra and g-string, she gently slipped a blindfold over my eyes.

In complete darkness, she led me to Jeremy, stopping me in front of him. They both began to caress me, and I was unable to differentiate between male and female hands.

"Kiss your Master's legs and chest," Annie whispered.

My lips touched his skin, alternating between wet kisses

and little bites. He reassured me that I was doing well and ordered me to run my hands over his underwear. Doing so, I felt proof of just how well I was doing. I could hear Annie and Jeremy kissing on the lips. The crotch of my catsuit was already soaked.

"Stand up, June," Annie commanded.

She tugged on my leash, leading me to a suspension bar where she attached my wrists and raised the bar. She then tied my ankles to two posts on either side of me.

Jeremy flogged my upper back, alternating between a cat-of-nine tails and a horsetail whip. Meanwhile, Annie worked her fingers over my crotch, and I realized that Jeremy had strategically cut holes in the catsuit. She slipped a finger through a tiny hole in the crotch and played with my clit.

"Don't come yet," she whispered.

Jeremy ordered her to rip the fabric and she began to tear at it until my entire pussy was exposed. She worked two fingers inside of me, moving them in and out, while Jeremy dug his fingers into the fabric and tore the back open.

He took Annie by her wrist-cuffs and attached her wrists to the bar, so that our bodies hung in suspension together. He continued to tear the fabric off of me until my breasts were exposed. Annie's bra had been removed at some point and she thrust her pendulous breasts into my small, pointy ones. I bent my head down and licked them.

Once the fabric had been entirely removed from my body, I was freed from suspension, still blindfolded.

"I'm going to teach you how to properly undress your Master. Get down on your knees," Annie commanded.

Kneeling, I searched for his skin with my hands.

"Slowly," she ordered. I did as told, taking my time and eventually undressing him. My fingers grazed his cock and I kissed his stomach. For some reason his penis seemed larger than it ever had. *Penis enlarger?* I asked myself.

"Stroke his cock," Annie insisted, and I responded by languishing over his cock with both hands. She could have told me to do anything and chances are, I'd have done it. She'd make an excellent cult leader.

I ran my tongue down his shaft and brought my lips to the tip where I tasted him. Finally I took him in my mouth.

"Take it all for your Master," she instructed.

I did as told and I'm not sure what Jeremy was doing to Annie but she was moaning right along with him.

Soon their hands were all over me. They made comments about the gushing state of my pussy. Its juices were dripping down my legs.

Next, they told me to bend over the leather bed at the center of the room. They led me to it and bending over I thrust my ass out so they could give it a good spanking.

"Get up on the bed," Jeremy instructed, helping me up where I was told to lie on my back. My wrists were cuffed to posts over my head and my legs were tied in the air, spread eagle, to posts at either side of the bed. My two instructors mounted me, and I think, although my eyes were incapacitated, that the two gave each other oral sex over my inert body.

Annie's shaved pussy landed on my lips as she straddled my face.

"Lick my pussy," she said and again, she said it sweetly so that it seemed in no way crass.

Jeremy then chained Annie's wrists to a post over the bed so she was just a bit higher up than before, and I had to crane my head in order to satisfy her. She moaned, and I thought maybe she came. I was so caught up in what I was doing to Annie, that I barely realized Jeremy doing his best to bring me to orgasm. His fingers were working on my g-spot and his tongue was on my clit.

Annie climbed off of me, and all I could feel was a multitude of limbs and hands on my skin. Cold chains tickled me, and fingernails dug into me. Gasps of pleasure filled the room. I heard someone unwrap a condom, and in complete darkness I felt skin, tongues, stubble, hair and teeth.

"Do you want to come?" Jeremy asked.

"Yes, Sir," I moaned.

"Do you want me to fuck you?"

"Yes, Sir."

"Say it."

"Please fuck me, Sir."

Jeremy entered me deftly, although with my legs tied spread eagle I was an easy target. Annie played with my tits while he moved inside of me. Delirious, I reached climax before Jeremy, due to the fact that I had four hands, two tongues and one penis stimulating me, and he only had one vagina—that's not to put down my vagina, or to say that *he* had a vagina. It's just that my vagina had been over-stimulated to a point of no return.

And though I'm not a screamer, it was so intense that I screamed.

Jeremy continued pounding me until I came again.

Shortly after my second orgasm, he came, then waited a moment and rolled off of me. I removed the blindfold slowly, hesitant to return to reality. My eyes struggled to adjust to the yellow light. Exhausted, I climbed off the bed and put on my dress.

Annie and I cleaned up while Jeremy showered (in Avalon's convenient and luxurious bathroom) so he wouldn't smell like pussy-juice and lube upon his return to the office.

When he emerged, dressed in a suit and smelling like Dial we led him to the elevator and said goodbye. Annie had a session immediately after. She did far more sessions than me since her standard of living was much higher. I wasn't trying to make millions, just pay my rent and buy beer, art supplies and food. So I kissed Annie goodbye and headed back downtown.

I always chose to walk back downtown even after it got cold. Usually I was so anxious to leave the dungeon, I did so with moisture still between my thighs. I'd race through midtown, eager to get to the Lower East Side. Sometimes, I felt envious of the various normals I passed, wondering if I'd ever have an ordinary job, a husband, kid, house or even a houseplant. The answer I realized was probably no. I didn't want these things. I'd *never* wanted these things. But the thing I wanted—to make art all day long—without being a slave, seemed almost entirely out of reach.

## Chapter 12

## *Femme Fatale*

Everybody asked me the same thing—*How long are you gonna do it?* I always had the same answer—*I'm gonna do it until I can afford not to.* I imagined I'd get a gallery show someday only I never sent out slides of my paintings. Other times, I imagined I'd get a writing gig. Tommy even offered to show my work to editors at some of the magazines he wrote for, but I was still too insecure to show my essays to anyone. It wasn't success I was afraid of; it was rejection. So I just kept going to the dungeon and daydreaming.

Many hours were spent lounging around the break room, killing time between sessions and waiting for prospective clients while getting to know the Mistresses. Each, it seemed, had a specialty. Anastasia was good with a bullwhip. Constantine was an expert at cock 'n' ball torture. Natasha was so Amazonian that she masqueraded as a Drag Queen and saw men who thought *she* was a man. It was like *Victor Victoria* or something. Sylvia, an older Dom, gave clients "brown showers." Gross, yes, but I was letting people beat me, so who was I to judge? Being in the midst of so many over-the-top females, I felt like I was living on Themyscira where Wonder Woman was born. A lot of time was spent getting ready with the Mistresses, helping them lace up corsets while they taught me the intricacy of makeup application. I began to transform from an asexual tomboy into a tomboy/Drag Queen. I grew my hair longer till it was far past my shoulders and started to wear eyeliner and sometimes, lipstick. The effect was one of pure jailbait. Makeup was new to me. So were high heels, garters and even bras, which I'd never bothered wearing in the past.

"I'm tired of always being Mary Ann. I wanna be Ginger," I said to Tommy one night when he noticed my cat-eye liner.

"Alice, I hate to break this to you, but you've always had plenty of Ginger in you. She's just visible these days," he said.

I knew I'd finally become a woman when I managed to apply false eyelashes without gluing my eyes together. It was more momentous than getting my first period. (I can now apply them in the back of a moving vehicle.) I know plenty of guys like the "natural look" but I wanted to be glamorous for a change, to wear sparkly outfits, turn heads and enslave the entire male species (psychologically, anyway.) Of course there were still rare occasions when I just wanted to go out in my cords and Yoda t-shirt, but the grunge of my art school days was getting further behind me as the ass of my vintage cords was getting ready to split. And *finally* I had money for clothes, nothing designer or fancy, mind you. Mostly I bought vintage, which was still cheap at the time, playing into my jailbait façade with get-ups that would have made Hedwig blush—tube tops, '60s hot-pants, halters, micro-minis and platforms. I kind of looked like a cross between Cher Barbie and Jodie Foster in *Taxi Driver*.

"Oh, Jesus, you look like a pedophile's dream," Dylan said when I met up with her wearing a lavender mini-dress, white fishnets and red pumps. "It looks like you got lost in your wacky aunt's closet circa 1974 and started playing dress-up."

Aside from spending time getting dressed with the Mistresses, I also got to know the "house slaves." These were dudes who ran errands and acted as maids for us at no fee as long as we humiliated them. It wasn't unusual to arrive at work to find one such slave vacuuming naked. Sometimes we made them run out and get us lunch (their treat), ChapStick, Dr. Scholl's insoles, moisturizer and anything else we wanted. Occasionally the Mistresses wrote "Property of The Inferno" on both sides of the house slave's hands so he would be publicly humiliated upon paying. I tried to get the most out of these slaves so I made them run lines with me for a play Kyle was directing that he and I had written together. It was an adventure called "Pirates of the Gowanus" that we only managed to stage once. I had cast myself as the leading lusty wench and had the house slaves do the lines of all the other parts from Blackbeard to the Cabin Boy to a friendly Sea Monster. I can honestly say I worked the house slaves harder than anyone else, which is funny because I wasn't even a Mistress.

One night I was lingering in the break-room when Anastasia, a Russian Dom with sandy blond hair and a body like a Bond Girl, emerged from the Quelle Fromage room wearing a black latex dress, spiked heels and a painted-on beauty mark. She scared me—a total "ice queen" who was in constant demand and who didn't talk much, possibly because English was her second language. She told Scarlet that her regular, Joseph, wanted an extra thirty minutes with an additional girl—a sub. They looked at me, the only sub. Anastasia intimidated the shit out of me. If we were on Themyscira, she was Wonder Woman (albeit blond and Russian.)

"Sure, I'll do it," I said, frightened more of letting her down than anything else.

"Good. Hurry up though. You don't need to get dressed up. Just black thong, black thigh-highs and heels. No top."

I changed in one minute flat.

"Perrrrfect," she said, fastening a collar and leash around my neck.

"I'm freezing!" Being topless in the hallway was cold.

I had no idea what to expect but when we got to the door, she started giggling. I had never seen her laugh before.

"You gonna love this," she said, busting open the door.

Joseph looked to be in his early fifties, slender with graying hair, he wore only a pair of blue manties. His wrists were chained to two posts above his head and his ankles were tied to two posts on the floor. The entire room reeked of pot smoke. It was like Spicoli's van in *Fast Times at Ridgemont High*. The radio was tuned to classic rock. A Steely Dan song played.

"Do you know VOT this FUCKING HIPPIE VOS doing in here before the session EVEN started?" Anastasia bellowed. Her accent's severity had doubled since we entered the room. She sounded like Dracula meets Natasha Fatale.

"No, Mistress."

"He VOS SMOKING POT!" At this, she gave his ass a smack with her hand. "Joseph, theees is June," she continued calmly. "Isn't she BEAUTIFUL?"

"Yes, Mistress."

She gently led me over to Joseph and placed me directly in front of him. He gazed longingly at my nipples.

"Do you vanna touch her?" she asked.

"Yes, Mistress."

"TOO FUCKING BAD!" She screamed and began another furious assault on his ass while he danced around in his chains.

"She is much better slave than you'll ever be because she doesn't do *illegal* drugs before session. Does your vife know you smoke pot?"

"No," he said meekly.

"Vell, if you don't behave, I call her and tell her about our sessions. Don't think I can't get her number."

He pleaded mercy and Anastasia promised that if he were very good, she would not call. Being "good" meant taking twenty spankings from me, which she told me I should deliver with force. If he "took them" and thanked me, not only would he get to touch my nipples; he might get to kiss them too.

I spanked him lightly at first.

"Harder, June!" Anastasia commanded. Not wanting to incur her wrath I spanked harder until there were handprints on Joseph's bony ass. He counted and thanked me, as

I had done so often for others. I felt a kinship with him, not just because he enjoyed a good spanking, but also because he was obviously a stoner like so many of my friends.

Once he'd taken twenty, he politely asked if he could touch my nipples.

"June, he used the magic word," Anastasia said, urging me toward him. Joseph timidly caressed my nipples and I felt a shiver of excitement. He then made the fatal mistake of running his tongue along my neck. Anastasia went ballistic.

"Did I TELL you that you could lick my slave?" she screamed.

She grabbed her riding crop and began to abuse his ass with it. Tears welled up in his eyes, maybe from the pot smoke, maybe from pain. Either way, they were coupled with a look of sheer ecstasy and a boner threatening to bust through his manties like the Incredible Hulk.

The sessions with Annie had been so heavy and serious that I'd forgotten one simple thing—sex is supposed to be fun whether it's kinky sex or just fucking in a bed. Anastasia who'd seemed so icy and cold *knew* this. She was a great terrible actress. She knew how to *play* and once she felt that Joseph had taken enough, she told him he could now play with me.

She untied him and had him fetch two small cuffs, which she attached to my wrists. Using rope, she tied the cuffs to the two gold pillars across from the room's large, gilded mirror. The cheesy cupid fountain trickled behind me. I couldn't help checking out my reflection in the fancy mirror since it was massive and directly across from me. I was in the crucifixion pose, my arms stretched out at my sides. My ribs stuck out and my stomach protruded slightly. *How did I get here?* I wondered—not just here on this planet, but more specifically, tied to two gold pillars, half-naked, in a midtown dungeon.

Anastasia then slipped a blindfold over my eyes before granting Joseph permission to caress and kiss me. He ran his hands and tongue over my skin, my nipples and between my thighs while Anastasia "tormented" both of us with the crop.

I was in Heaven. Anastasia was a Femme Fatale and Joseph was a kindly, aging hippie with a good touch. Orgasm didn't seem to be the goal, just wild sensory experience and theater. *This is the way sessions should be*, I thought.

At precisely that moment, Anastasia removed my blindfold and told me the session was over. No one had an orgasm and no one asked for more. Joseph appeared satisfied though I imagine he probably ran home and beat off like a madman.

I helped Anastasia coil up the rope into neat little bundles while Joseph dressed. Afterwards, he opened his wallet and tipped us each sixty bucks. Then, to my shock, he handed us each a *massive* bag of pot, the likes of which I had only seen in documentaries about drug cartels. Later, Kyle estimated it was worth about three hundred bucks.

I was speechless as we said goodbye.

"He grows his own," Anastasia whispered as we slinked back to the dressing room with our contraband tip.

I saw Joseph a few more times, sometimes with Anastasia, sometimes without. The times I saw him alone, he dominated me. We smoked weed and drank wine throughout and he always tipped me the same thing—an alarmingly massive bag of pot.

He quickly became my favorite client. When Kyle saw the first bag of weed Joseph gave me, he began to rethink his stance on my job the dungeon.

"Maybe," he said, inhaling deeply on the bright green bud, "It's not that bad."

## Chapter 13

## *As High as the Billboards*

Tommy called from a payphone in midtown.

"Come meet me at Rudy's. It's nothin' but old men here, drinking and staring straight ahead. It's great."

Rudy's was (and is) a Hell's Kitchen bar that hadn't become trendy yet because Hell's Kitchen (the Manhattan neighborhood between 34th and 59th, west of 8th Avenue) hadn't become trendy yet. Rudy's opened in 1933 and was one of the first joints in New York to be granted a liquor license after Prohibition ended. Tommy and I liked it because they served cheap pitchers there and because a six-foot-tall pig statue sat out front. According to legend, the pig was stolen twice before they bolted its ass down. The other great thing about Rudy's is that it was never too crowded, especially during the day, which was when Tommy and I most often drank there. He'd taken a temporary admin job for one of the networks whose offices were in a nearby Times Square high-rise. He hated everything about it—his coworkers, his assignments and the hours. About the only thing he liked was the job's proximity to Rudy's.

It was a Friday afternoon and I was doing nothing but

working on a painting of Jake, my roommate, as Pan the goat-legged God. Jake was tired of posing and I was tired of painting. Rudy's seemed like the perfect alternative, albeit a possible road to a lost weekend.

I hopped the F Train and headed uptown where I found Tommy sitting at the bar alongside the aforementioned old men. There were about a dozen of them, all silently staring straight ahead, not at a television but at the shelf of booze just out of their reach. They didn't seem depressed. It was more like they were meditating.

"Dude!" Tommy hollered when he saw me, jumping up from his stool and hugging me. "Thank Jesus H. Christ you are here. I *had* to leave work. Those people are turning me into a complete, unadulterated alcoholic as if I weren't bad enough already."

"Well, this is a nice break from the 'Coolitis Epidemic' on Ludlow."

*Coolitis* was what Tommy and I called the obsession with being cool so many hipsters suffered from throughout the city, especially on the Lower East Side.

We ordered a pitcher of Becks for only six bucks, the going rate for a single beer in plenty of other bars, and took it out back to Rudy's dilapidated patio where we waxed poetic about being visionary underachievers.

"These women I work with, they're newly married and they've all got these hyphenated names. They have three names and I've still got the name I had when was twelve. I'm not even a Tom yet. I'm still a Tommy. It makes me feel like a child."

"I sometimes feel like a teen runaway. Maybe Covenant House would take me in."

"Maybe they'll take us both in after I quit my job and get evicted. Speaking of which, they actually gave me keys to the office so after we down a couple of these I say we go over there and make ourselves comfy. Great view, big couches and cable."

"I haven't seen cable TV since I left my parent's house. All I watch is Charlie Rose."

We downed our first pitcher while discussing screenplays we'd never get around to actualizing. Tommy wanted to write one called "Animal Avengers" where we play animal rescue workers who go around beating the shit out of cruel humans in order to save adorable animals.

"It would culminate in us accidentally killing an abusive Chihuahua owner," Tommy said, "And what follows would be a road trip where we're running from the Man—an uncool *Wild at Heart* with a crazy Chihuahua in the backseat! It would be awesome and you'd have to learn karate because it would be *so gratifyin*g to watch you kick ass."

"We should write it."

"Absolutely, but first we should get another pitcher."

Following our second pitcher we walked through Times Square, stopping along the way to pick up a six-pack then stopping again to pet the police horses before making our way to Tommy's office.

"Welcome to the Dark Tower of Mordor," he said as we entered and rode the elevator to the forty-first floor. It was after seven so the place was empty.

"Get comfortable and *please* steal whatever office supplies you need," he added, dropping pens into my purse. "Do you need a stapler?"

We walked by his desk and he said that when his co-workers took his chair, he simply sat on the floor. He then physically demonstrated how he does this, plopping down on the floor and dramatically reaching his hands up to his desk to type and take calls.

Finally we went to the lounge where we lay on massive couches, popped open our beers and watched cable on the big screen TV, channel-surfing, as only two people deprived of cable can. Finally, we settled on switching between a Sinbad comedy special and a documentary on Calvin Klein. When we ran out of beer and it was almost time to go, Tommy then led me to a conference room with a spectacular view of Times Square—the giant outdoor TV screen flanked by a billboard ad for Budweiser and a huge ad for Ramen Noodles that was shaped like a cup of them with fake steam coming out of it.

"Ramen and Bud—the two things that sustained me throughout early adulthood," I noted.

Alongside the Bud and Ramen, there were underwear, music and movie ads. Underneath it all were hordes of tiny ant-people busily running around, looking for action—the physical opposite of the men at Rudy's.

I was thinking, *this is what New York City is all about,* when I turned to Tommy. He had a look in his eye that matched my own, a gleam of insanity and excitement at being part of the swirling chaos of New York City, of stealing pens and ditching work and drinking beer in bars guarded by porcelain pigs with a history more sordid than our own. We were quiet for the first time that afternoon, studying each other and recognizing this in each other, when suddenly Tommy kissed me, a great big romantic kiss. An instant later we were kissing madly, devouring each other with stale beer breath and joy. Soon we were on the ground, pulling each other's clothes off.

"Are there security cameras in here?" I asked.

"Do you care?"

"No."

"Me neither."

My top was off, my panties were on the floor and my skirt was around my waist. Tommy grabbed a condom from his bag, slipped it on and right there on the floor of a conference room in Times Square, we fucked, as high up as the giant billboards. *This* was what New York was all about.

## Chapter 14

## *The Achilles' Heel of Wall Street*

After Tommy and I had our conference room tryst, we agreed to just "be friends", albeit friends who knew what it was like to fuck on the floor of a network television conference room, possibly in front of security cameras. We were obviously extremely attracted to each other but we also had a deep, abiding respect and love for each other, a respect and love that meant we weren't about to ruin each other with an emotionally draining relationship.

Plus, our lives were a mess. Tommy was a struggling freelance writer, aspiring comedian and temp who chose *not* to temp most days and I was a sub who was getting increasingly entangled in the world of S&M. As I did, I met more professionals in the field. At some point, Annie introduced me to a "psychosexual counselor" named Anya who ran a program where clients could receive both analysis and "erotic services." On the surface, this seemed like a great idea since plenty of the men I'd seen at the dungeon could have benefited from therapy. But the reality of what happened at Anya's was that she would talk to the "patient" for about ten minutes in her office then he would see a Mistress or sub for an hour in a room that looked an awful lot like a small dungeon. Anya would then (like any pimp) reap most of the profits. Still, working for a psychoanalyst felt a touch less sleazy than working at a dungeon so I started doing a couple sessions a month at Anya's Madison Avenue office.

Anya was in her fifties when I met her and though I was never sure if she had a shrink's credentials she had a history that could fill volumes. She was born to wealthy bohemian parents in Sweden and lived in a number of European countries. At puberty, she sprouted long legs, immense breasts and a rebellious streak that even her liberal family couldn't contain. At eighteen, she headed west and from my short conversations with her, I learned that, at various times in her life, she had worked as a call girl in Cuba, a bunny at a Playboy Club, a nude model, stripper and porn star in California and eventually, a Dominatrix in New York City. That's when she became interested in and started studying psychosexual problems. There were several diplomas hanging around her office, one of which was a PhD in human sexuality. Like most therapists, Anya was insane.

The majority of clients she tossed my way were leg and foot fetishists who couldn't come unless a leg or foot was involved in the equation. I didn't give "foot jobs" but I did, on more than one occasion, let a gentleman jizz on my stockings while I pretended to be a schoolgirl riding the subway at rush hour. This was a scenario constructed by Anya for what purposes I'll never know.

One night I was sitting in Anya's dressing room with Jesse, a male cross-dressing Mistress I'd just met. He was new to the fetish scene and he moved with incredible grace. His makeup was impeccably applied and despite being a foot taller than me, he was ten times more feminine than I'll ever be. I watched him slowly unpack his bag, and as he did, he unraveled an extra-long, lace-trimmed, thigh-high stocking.

"The power of this one tiny piece of fabric," he said.

"It's like Kryptonite to Superman."

"The Achilles' heel of Wall Street."

Jesse was correct. I had watched many a seemingly invulnerable banker turn immediately Kryptonian upon catching a glimpse of my thigh-high-clad legs. But all men are different. To find a man's fetish is to find his weakness, and to know the power of the smallest details. I had already learned the power of thigh-highs, but also the power of white cotton panties, of Tinker Bell perfume, of collars, of thongs, of poorly applied red lipstick, of freckles, of two white knee socks worn in disarray (one up and one down) on purpose, of gloves, leather, lace and a host of other things contained in Stevie Nicks' songs. And, later that night, I understood the power of black patent-leather mary janes so polished I could see a fragmented, liquefied reflection of my face in them as I bent over the wooden horse awaiting Ethan, a young Englishman who had come to Anya for "therapy."

Often, Anya told me very little about the men I was about to see. Ethan, she told me, wanted to see me cry. I was to be bent over the horse when he arrived whereupon he would spank me, but the tears, she reminded me, were the most important part. That's it. He had just flown in, and Anya's was his first stop on a short business trip.

I remained bent over the horse as I heard Ethan close

the door to the tiny room. His footsteps approached, but I remained perfectly still. His hands pressed gently against the wool fabric of my gray schoolgirl skirt and he moved them around, inspecting my "assets."

"You can stand up now," he said in the kind of British accent that leaves not a dry vagina in the house. I stood up and turned to face him. To my surprise, his face was almost as lovely as his accent—high cheekbones, square jaw, black eyes and brown hair that hung sloppily over his eyes. In contrast to his scruffy hair, his clothes were immaculate—a tailored navy suit and white shirt. But it was his black eyes that got me, the kind of eyes that don't reflect anything, so full of secrets they never sparkle. I had ceased to be turned on by most sessions at that point but with Ethan, I was both fascinated *and* turned on. How many women, I wondered had he tormented through the years? How many women had been unable to understand his fetishes?

"I am going to spank you," he said abruptly. "And, I want you to tell me when you are about to cry. It is very important that you be honest and that you really cry."

"Yes, Sir."

Moisture was already beginning to soak through my panties as he motioned for me to bend over the horse again. I bent over slowly, sticking my bottom out, inviting him, whereupon he began to spank me relentlessly. My ass stung and I closed my eyes, wondering if he could tell how wet I was. The spanking was unrelenting and he never slowed down. He didn't apologize. Didn't ask me if it was too hard. It *was* too hard, but for the first time ever, I wanted it *harder*.

I stuck my ass out further, feeling as if I might die if he didn't rip my panties off and shove his cock into me. I couldn't see him, didn't dare turn around, but I knew he must be hard. He stood at a distance, didn't try to touch my pussy, didn't try to grab my breasts—all the usual stunts clients pulled.

I wanted to beg him, "*Please* fuck me. I can't take this," but I was afraid to make a sound. The room was completely quiet except for the sound of his hand spanking my ass. There was no role-play, no dialogue, nothing for me to say. I felt like I was on the brink of coming and he had barely touched me.

The spanking continued for about fifteen minutes when finally the pain became so intense that I thought I might cry. I was embarrassed to tell him yet he instinctively knew.

"Are you going to cry?" he asked.

"Yes."

He leaned in closer in order to watch me, but he continued spanking me as he did. I then did something that wasn't in Anya's instructions, something submissives generally aren't supposed to do—I looked directly in his eyes. In that moment, all of the secrets held in them fell away, and amidst all of the playacting, I glimpsed the eyes of an expectant child about to get their wish.

He took a break from spanking me to unzip his trousers and take out what I had correctly presumed was an enormous erection. He then recommenced spanking me with one hand while he stroked his cock with his other. Soon thereafter, I started to cry. He reached out his finger and lightly touched my cheek for a millisecond withdrawing it quickly as though he had just committed some horrible transgression. His breathing grew harder and in a few seconds, he came.

I was *soaked*, more turned on than I'd ever been in a session yet Ethan was totally uninterested in fucking me. *He only wanted to see me cry.* That was enough. *Did he have girlfriends?* I wondered. And, if he did, did they participate in this sort of scenario? I couldn't get it out of my mind.

The end of a session was always slightly uncomfortable, handing clients baby wipes and paper towels and anything else they required to clean the cum from their person, but with Ethan it was doubly uncomfortable given the intensity of what had just occurred and the fact that we'd barely spoken.

He thanked me, handed me a decent tip and left.

The session hadn't even lasted thirty minutes, but I wanted it to continue. I wanted to say to him, "I have enough tears to give you a permanent erection but from now on, when you come, come inside me." But I never said that. I never said anything. And I never saw him again.

# Chapter 15

## *Just Stay Alive*

There are only two kinds of phone calls that happen after midnight—bad ones and booty calls. I had just drifted off to sleep at about 2 A.M., after a night of sober painting when the phone rang. Unfortunately, it wasn't a booty call.

Kyle was calling from Saint Vincent's Hospital. He was about to be admitted to the psych ward for an involuntary, extended vacay.

Two days earlier, he'd discovered that Jessicunt had been cheating on him with an old friend of his for over a month. This explained a lot including the fact that he'd mysteriously contracted the Clap from his supposedly monogamous girlfriend. Not surprisingly, a bitter breakup ensued.

The betrayal, the breakup and the Clap plunged him into a heavy state of despair whereupon he called his shrink and made the mistake of telling her he felt suicidal.

"I only said I *felt* suicidal. I didn't say I *was* suicidal!" he exclaimed.

"Kyle, you can *never* use that word around shrinks. They make sure you get locked up or it's their ass."

The shrink insisted Kyle go to the hospital where they were preparing to lock him up for a minimum of seventy-two hours. Because he had two six-month-old kittens, he insisted they let him call someone to care for them. If anything happened to his kittens, he said, he really would kill himself.

Jake was awake when I got the call. He was running around the kitchen manically measuring my paintings because he was determined to get me an art show. He also had a pot of rice and beans cooking on the stove as if it were six P.M.

"What's going on?" he asked.

"Kyle is about to get locked up in the nuthouse and I either gotta bust him out or I gotta get his keys and take care of Frodo and Troll."

"Where is he?"

"St. Vincent's. Wanna come?"

"Sure."

My body ached from work. My throat was swollen as if I was about to get sick, but there was no way in hell I wasn't going. Kyle was my best friend and I knew that he'd do the same for me, that he'd probably *have* to do the same for me at some point. I don't know a single decent artist who's never visited the nuthouse.

We hopped in a cab and raced to St. Vincent's in the West Village, not far from the apartment where Kyle lived. The waiting room was a sad scene as always, full of people who looked like they were in physical and mental anguish with the exception of two rough looking trannies who were having a grand old time. They passed a flask back and forth while providing commentary on all waiting room activities.

"Awww…what a cute couple!" one of them exclaimed when Jake and I walked in.

"We're just roommates," I said.

"Uh huh, girl…sure."

The trannies introduced themselves as Coco and Lisa. Coco immediately told me I looked like Courteney Cox and asked what we were doing there.

"Here for a friend," I said, afraid to ask what she was doing there.

Realizing it was going to be a long night, Jake ran out and bought beers, which he poured into coffee cups so as not to arouse the suspicions of St. Vincent's security.

"Look at them drinkin' coffee at this hour!" Lisa disdainfully announced upon his return. We sipped our beers until a nurse told us that one of us could go see Kyle while he was being "evaluated." She led me to a curtained-off room where he was sitting on a bed wearing only a backless, paper gown of shame and a look of extreme anxiety.

"Alice, you have *got* to get me out of here," he said. "I'm not crazy and I'm not gonna kill myself. I don't belong here. Who knew they'd take everything so literally?"

"Where's all your stuff?"

"They took it so I don't hang myself with my belt. I don't even have my shoes lest I off myself with shoelaces."

"Jesus. Okay. I gotta get your things and then I'll see if I can sneak you out, but you've got to promise me one thing."

"What?"

"Just stay alive."

"Like the Bee Gees."

"The Brothers Gibb knew all."

At that point, a female doctor approached and said I'd have to wait outside until Kyle's evaluation was complete. I asked for his keys and she handed me a bag containing everything Kyle had been wearing that evening.

"Damn! Your friend's got some *big* feet," Coco said when she noticed Kyle's size twelve shoes sticking out of the bag.

"Oh my *God!* When does he get out?" Lisa added.

Meanwhile, Jake had joined in on the fun, assisting in their harassment of the hunky EMT guys who passed by.

"Mr. EMT, I think my water just broke!" Coco shouted.

Jake suggested they yell, "Mr. EMT, I fell and I need you to cut my clothes off."

"Good one!" Coco said, taking a swig from her flask. She then inexplicably stood up and asked the entire waiting room, "Who was the best Catwoman?"

"Julie Newmar," I answered, which was apparently the right answer, as Coco then high-fived me, almost knocking me to the ground.

"I need pills!" Lisa then screamed to no one in particular.

After over two hours of hangin' with Coco and Lisa, a nurse told me I could say goodbye to Kyle. They were, as expected, going to lock him up for three days.

I found Kyle sitting up on his gurney, looking completely sane and ready to go.

"You're gonna have to help me go all 'Chief' Bromden here cuz I am *not* about to be subjected to the Cuckoo's Nest," he said.

"I don't see any windows or hydrotherapy consoles."

"Well, they're not gonna let me go and I know that staying will *make* me insane."

We noticed what looked like a side exit and Kyle suggested we might be able to sneak through it even though it was guarded and he was barefoot and wearing an ass-less paper gown.

"We've at least got to try," he pleaded.

"OK. Jake's got your stuff in case anything happens."

We waited till the doctors weren't looking whereupon Kyle hopped up from his gurney and we attempted to run out. We made it through the first set of automatic doors when security grabbed us. They only got a piece of my arm and I wriggled free but two big guards grabbed Kyle and roughly dragged him back inside kicking and screaming. Shut out, I was told never to return.

"I'll take care of your kittens!" I shouted after Kyle.

Jake, Coco and Lisa had witnessed our valiant effort and Jake came outside to meet me with the bag of Kyle's belongings.

"Coco and Lisa wanted me to say goodbye. They were still trying to get Lisa some Valium," Jake said.

"That place could drive anybody to need a Valium."

It was now close to dawn as Jake and I quietly walked the few blocks to Kyle's place, a gorgeous one-bedroom in a West Village brownstone. Kyle was a born and bred New Yorker whose family had been smart enough to buy property in Manhattan when it was feasible hence he now paid less than three hundred bucks a month to live there.

"I think I'm gonna crash here and keep the cats company," I said when we arrived at his door.

"All right. I'm working the brunch shift tomorrow so I gotta get some z's."

"I'm worried about Kyle."

"Me too, but you know, they'll probably just drug him so he gets all catatonic then let him out once he's no longer interesting."

"You're right. I'm gonna try to visit him tomorrow. I might have to wear a disguise, but I'm gonna try anyway."

Inside, I fed the rambunctious kittens while noticing the grimy state of Kyle's formerly beautiful apartment. People usually react to depression in one of two ways—either they clean compulsively or not at all. It looked like Kyle hadn't cleaned or even opened his mail in weeks. I resolved to clean the next day, but at the moment could barely stand up. So as the long night turned into day, I curled up with the kittens and slept.

Because the psych ward was in a separate building from the waiting room, I wasn't recognized by security so I could visit. The first day of Kyle's stay, Tommy visited with me, bearing gifts of bagels and lox.

"I hate feeling like this," Kyle said, "I don't care about anything. It's like I've had a frontal lobotomy."

"I feel like I've had a bottle in front of me," Tommy said. "Seriously, I think I'm still drunk from last night."

I noticed an insanely beautiful girl talking with a woman who looked like her mom.

*"Who is that?"* I asked.

"Irene. She's a model. She moved here from Nebraska like three months ago and already tried to slit her wrists. She's so fucking hot, it's killing me."

"See. You're not a zombie, you still like crazy girls."

"And if she's *really* crazier than a shithouse condominium, she'll probably like you back," Tommy added.

"Well, she's super smart. She wants to be a pilot."

Just as Kyle was telling us about some of the psych ward's recreational activities—how they'd all watched *Mrs. Doubtfire* that morning—a nurse told us visiting hours were over. We hugged Kyle goodbye and he promised to save us some good drugs. I promised to bring him a bagel again the next day.

I'd told Tommy about the disastrous state of Kyle's apartment and he offered to help clean, so when we left, we swung by the bodega and stocked up on beer, Scrubbing Bubbles and Mr. Clean.

We set to work cleaning until the place was spotless. I even burned Native American sage to remove bad vibes while Tommy alphabetized Kyle's CD collection. We gave Frodo and Troll catnip and watched them get crazy. Finally, Tommy said, "You know what we ought to do?"

"What?"

"You ever penis-bomb someone?"

"No. What the fuck is that?"

"You basically cut up a bunch of tiny pieces of paper and then you *draw penises* on them and then you hide them *all over* the apartment. Then the person finds them for like a year. You put them everywhere, in CDs, in jacket pockets, in the pantry."

"We HAVE to. Genius!"

For the next two hours, Tommy and I drew and hid

penises all over Kyle's apartment, laughing hysterically the whole time. While hiding penises, Tommy stumbled upon Kyle's weed.

"Oh, Man! Weed! Do you think Kyle would mind?"

"Not if we just smoke a tiny bit."

We rolled a miniscule joint, which turned out to be *extremely* strong. Minutes later we were more baked than Frodo and Troll were on catnip. We lay down on Kyle's bed and started kissing, our resolve to be just friends gone for the night.

# Chapter 16

## *Hang My Hopes*

Kyle's "incarceration" lasted for three days. When he got home and saw his spotless apartment, he told me he cried with joy. Then he told me, when he started to find the penises, he laughed for hours. A year later, he still found penises. He'd go to get a tissue from a pocket and there would be a penis!

Meanwhile, Stu, who'd returned from his tour, began calling me again.

"Ugh. That is so *typical* of men," Dylan said over post-dungeon cocktails. "You start screwing someone else and they just start sniffin' around your skirt again."

"I've only slept with Tommy twice. We're still *just friends*."

"My ass! You're just 'friends.' You're his 'friend' who knows what it's like to have *his penis* pounding away inside of *your vagina* and he's *your friend* who knows what it's like to stick *his penis* inside of *your vagina* over and over and over again until you squirt female ejaculate all over his bed sheets and he sleeps in it for two weeks."

"We're very close friends."

"What are you afraid of?"

"Love."

"Why?"

"Because I hear it conquers all, and how can something that conquers all not be the most terrifying thing on the planet?"

"Maybe real love is what happens when you aren't afraid of being conquered. It's like putting your own shackles on because the conqueror is so beautiful you can't resist being its slave."

"I'm really kind of over being a slave to anyone or anything. Stu's emotional unavailability is comforting."

"There'll come a time when that unavailability, when his Triple Gemini bullshit, ceases to makes your pussy wet. You're gonna get bored."

"I'm bored with Stu's behavior, not his cock."

Dylan and I finished our drinks and headed over to Jake's open mike, a raucous show called "The Hoity-Toity." It was held weekly in the lounge of a swank hotel a few blocks from The Inferno. How Jake ever secured this space as a room for us Lower East Side freaks to gallivant in is beyond me. I'd brought along an essay I'd written about my first session with Pete, which I planned on reading.

When we arrived, a primal-scream-therapy performance artist was onstage, bent over, his pants around his ankles and his ass to the audience. He pulled his ass cheeks apart and screamed "Embarrassed!" repeatedly. The crowd loved it.

Stu, unsurprisingly, was there. In between tours and "real gigs" he used the open mike as a place to fuck around, play covers and work on new songs.

"Alice," he said, pulling me close and inhaling my hair.

"Coconuts. Your hair always smells like coconuts. I've missed it."

"You can get a bottle of it at the 99-cent store."

"I miss you," he slurred, staggering a bit. The fact that he was visibly drunk didn't stop me from answering in the affirmative when he asked quite simply, "Wanna fuck?" I appreciate questions that only require a yes or no answer.

We waited until after I read my essay, which was greeted with hoots and hollers, then hopped in a cab and sped down to his place on Avenue C, which he'd recently moved into with his bassist, Dan.

"You want some wine?" he asked, drunkenly attempting to open a bottle to no avail.

"Here," I said, pulling out two 24-ounce Budweisers I'd been carrying in my oversized purse. "No corkscrew required."

He opened his can and it exploded all over him. I opened mine and it exploded too.

"Sorry, been running around with them in there."

We went into his tiny room and I noticed the way he'd mounted a TV on the wall like it was a hospital room. He sat on the edge of his bed and I straddled and kissed him, the beer still in my right hand.

"What I love about you, Alice, is that you get right down to it," he said.

True. I don't like giving someone my resume before I fuck him. I don't care what you did today and I don't want you to care what I did. Be in the here and now with me.

We began to disrobe while kissing and miraculously not losing track of our beers.

"I think I'm the only one who really understands you, Alice."

"Great, because I don't understand me. Maybe you can explain me to me."

"You wanna know what I think? I think you're just a pretty girl who has made some bad choices."

I wasn't bothered by the fact that he'd reduced me to "pretty girl" since, at that moment, I'd reduced him to "broken alcoholic."

"It's the bad choices that have made my life worth living. Do you think I've set out to make *good* choices? On my deathbed, I won't be sitting there feeling satisfied because my life was so full of smart choices. I mean, I probably won't *have* a deathbed due to all the bad choices, but when it's time for me to go, I'll think, *my life was a train wreck, but at least it was a fun one.*"

"Am I one?"

"What?"

"A bad choice."

"You? You're an experience."

He kissed me and threw me down on the bed, a full fifteen ounces of Bud flying through the air as he pinned me beneath him.

"I love you. I mean it. I love you. Why do you always run away?" he asked.

I kissed him because I didn't want to say something angry like, "Because the last time you told me you loved me, you didn't call me for a month and during that time, I stopped caring."

"I mean it. I love you." He nuzzled his head in my hair, inhaling the chemical coconuts, as I unbuttoned the snaps on his western shirt. We rolled around, he pulled his pants off, I pulled my dress off and we fucked with surprising vigor given his inebriated state. I gave him head and he ate my pussy, stopping only to tell me he meant it, he really did love me.

After we'd both come buckets, he pulled out a pack of Camel Straights and lit two, one for him and one for me. He turned on the overhead hospital TV and we lay there naked, watching cartoons and smoking.

By morning, Stu was passed out cold. I made sure he was breathing then slipped out, walking home in the cool autumn air. I thought about Stu—all the times he'd stared down emotional, spiritual or artistic death, all the times he'd had writer's block or ennui or anxiety and decided to call me and all the times I picked up the phone and moments later appeared pantiless, drunk and open in his bedroom and we got naked and sweaty and spilled wine all over his sheets and he looked up from my pussy to tell me loved me.

I would never save Stu from himself; I could only participate in his destruction, which is why he'd never settle down with me. Someday a normal woman would come along and be his partner and he'd forget about me. She would do more than make sure he was breathing. She'd make toast and tea and babies and they'd paint their apartment together and have Woody Allen moments together while I continued an existence of bohemian extremism. I was as unavailable as Stu.

Maybe he *did* love me, but I didn't care. No matter how many times he uttered those three little words, I would never hang my hopes on him.

## Chapter 17

*Devoured*

Annie and I saw William, the Japanese businessman, a second time at Avalon. I wore pink cotton panties, a pink cardigan sweater, my gray Catholic schoolgirl skirt, bobby socks and pumps. There had been no heat or hot water in my building so my hair was an unwashed, tangled mess, tied up in a ponytail. I tried to layer on deodorant in an attempt to mask my overripe scent, but ran out after the first stroke, so I went natural instead. At sessions, I never used perfume or even moisturizer because I didn't think clients wanted to go back to work or home to their wives smelling like enchanted apples or tea rose. But with William, how I looked hardly seemed an issue. Costumes were never important to him.

Moments after we greeted him, he told us to remove our clothes. We quickly stripped buck naked, which felt totally unerotic. There is nothing sexier than the slow unraveling of a thigh-high, the unsnapping of a bra, or the unbuttoning of a cardigan. I know I'm hot for a man when I've memorized his belt buckle. I even like the awkward shoe removal that transpires before sex. If I'm in love, I even like the smell of my lover's socks.

We stood in front of William who was also naked. His

penis was already hard and he was "all smiles" as he went about his brand of creative sadism.

First he pulled two heavy, hardcover, encyclopedia-size books down from the bookshelf in "the library." He then instructed us to put our hands at our sides and to balance the books on our heads. Whoever dropped the book first would be the recipient of torture. Annie and I placed the books on our heads and tried to stand perfectly still, as he twisted our nipples and spanked our bottoms. Finally, Annie flinched, and her book came tumbling down. I beamed with joy since Annie had won every challenge in our last session with William.

William then told me to get a cup of ice from the kitchen.

"What should we do with the ice?" he asked me.

"We should put it inside of her."

Annie looked horrified, but in my delusional mind, I thought she might enjoy it. I remembered one boyfriend, who, in the sweltering heat, would run ice cubes over my naked body. I would then take an ice cube, and put it inside of me whereupon he would thrust in and out of me—hot, cold, hot, cold—until the ice melted. Some people stay cool by sitting in front of a fan in an un-air-conditioned apartment in the middle of July, but I always opted for this method.

However, that was mid-July, and this was mid-March, and while we were in a heated room, the very idea of ice coming into contact with her pussy made Annie cringe.

I stealthily snuck through Avalon's hallway naked and retrieved a cup of ice from the kitchen. When I returned, Annie was lying on the leather bed, a wee-wee pad under her ass. She took an ice cube, put it inside a condom and slowly began to insert it. By the time it disappeared inside her, she was covered in beads of sweat.

William then switched gears, abruptly requesting a little foot worship. We got down on all fours and kissed his feet as he spanked us with a leather paddle. Moments later, he told us to stand up and face each other. When we did, he produced two large nipple clamps and affixed them to our right nipples. He then somehow produced a piece of yellow string, which he used to attach the nipple clamps to each other. On the ground between Annie and me, he placed a paper towel.

"We're going to have a tug-of-war!" he announced. "Whoever crosses this line will lose," he added, pointing to the paper towel.

This was going to be my comeuppance for the ice scenario since I loathe nipple torture and Annie clearly loved it. Plus, her breasts were twice the size of mine. As she began to pull, I feared my entire mammary gland would become detached from my body. I mouthed the word "bitch" to Annie who smiled.

Finally, I said, "I surrender before I lose what little breasts I have." Stepping over the paper towel, I accepted defeat. It was like a perverse episode of *Survivor*.

William told me to lie down on the leather bed. I did as instructed and he cuffed my wrists and ankles to the bed so I couldn't move. Meanwhile, Annie blindfolded me so I wouldn't know what was coming next. From this point on, I couldn't tell which hands were performing which act, the exception being when Annie stroked my hair and I recognized her gentle touch.

Nipple clamps were soon attached to my already sore nipples. I then felt a device called a "Wartenberg Wheel" trailing across my belly. The Wartenberg Wheel was originally designed by Dr. Robert Wartenberg to test nerve reactions, as it is rolled systematically across the skin. It has since been adopted by the BDSM community as a wacky toy used for sexual hijinks. The small wheel, which sits at the end of a short, usually stainless steel handle, features sharp, radiating pins that rotate around when rolled across the flesh. While not sharp enough to pierce the skin unless excessive force is used, they occasionally hurt like a motherfucker, especially when you're tied up and wearing heavy nipple clamps.

But that was just the beginning. In case you're wondering what happened to the rest of the ice I retrieved from the kitchen, pretty soon a large ice cube, a mini-glacier of sorts, was thrust inside my pussy.

*Is it possible to get frostbite on one's vagina?* I panicked.

One set of hands then dumped the rest of the ice on my skin and trailed the various cubes up and down my body while the other set of hands lit a candle. I know because I heard matches being lit and smelled the scent of sulfur and dripping candle wax. Seconds later, a torrent of *hot* wax poured onto my *freezing* skin.

The prickling wheel, the ice, the wax and the nipple clamps sent me into a transcendental state wherein my etheric body said "fuck this" and began to climb out of my physical body. But then, a vibrator set at full speed was thrust against my clit, and I was forced out of my momentary transcendence, not by sexual arousal but by a neurotic fear of electrocution, given the close proximity of the ice to the electrical vibrator.

Just as I became convinced that I was about to die one of the lamest deaths in history, the two sadists turned off the vibrator, untied me and undid my blindfold. My stomach was covered in so much lavender wax. I looked like an alien temporarily having a terrible visit to this planet.

I'd been so far from reality it took a second to kick in. Once it did, I was thrust back into surreality as William again commanded Annie and me to stand with the books on our heads. We did as told and this time he paddled us hard. My equilibrium was destroyed and after three strokes, I flinched and my book came tumbling down.

Annie had certainly exacted her revenge for the earlier ice incident and now it was simply gratuitous. They scooted a small, leather table under the doorway and instructed me to lie down on it whereupon they cuffed my wrists and ankles to its shackles. Annie then unexpectedly pulled two mousetraps out of her bag of tricks. These she clamped to my nipples. She then tied the mousetraps together using a long piece of yellow string, which she tied to an eyehook at the top of the doorway. This made the mousetraps stand erect so that anytime anyone so much as grazed the string it sent waves of pain through my upper body.

Stranger still, Annie pulled out two plastic, yellow, monkey-shaped clothespins. These she attached to my labia, which didn't hurt at all. It was actually quite pleasant, but then she tied the little monkeys together using another piece of yellow string, which she attached to the eyehook at the top of the door.

William then attempted to put wooden clothespins on the flesh above my armpits. This was my limit. After a second I screamed, "Mercy!" and he removed them.

Once I was in this position—nipples attached to mousetraps attached to string attached to the top of the door frame, which was also attached to yellow, monkey clothespins attached to my labia—Annie and William began to tickle and finger me.

Next, William brought out a large dildo, draped in a condom, and told me to suck on it. Annie then blindfolded me and told me to play with myself with my right hand while I held the giant dildo, which I was still sucking, in my left hand. I did as instructed, but was nowhere close to coming. I was just too exhausted and there was simply too much going on to feel aroused. Plus, I really thought I might have vaginal frostbite. Because I was blindfolded, I couldn't see what Annie and William were doing. William was moaning, so I assumed he was likely jerking off, receiving a hand job, or receiving a blowjob. Moments later, I heard William make orgasmic noises until I was pretty sure he'd reached the big O and I could stop sucking on the dildo.

A minute later, Annie removed my blindfold. I looked down at my immobilized body, and the yellow string woven across it, attaching me to the door. I felt like a small insect caught in a spider's web, about to be devoured. *Maybe,* I thought, *I already have been.*

## Chapter 18

## *Catholic Bush*

Months passed and my Rolodex grew fat with pervs, some likeable, some loathsome and some totally off the wall. There was Fred, who had a love/hate relationship with pubic hair. It was his reason for living yet he was completely fixated on its removal. Annie had introduced me to him for one simple reason—I was one of the last remaining women in the sex industry to still sport pubic hair. At the time, I had a well-trimmed bush—not a landing strip, not waxed, just a neat, full pelvic region of hair—unusual in the sex industry where bald or partially bald is now the preferred aesthetic. With my long hippie hair and my retro pubes, I kind of looked like an illustration in the original *Joy of Sex*.

(Eventually, I let another pube-obsessed client shave my vulva and I realized I enjoyed being hairless since a shaved pussy is more exposed for titillation hence getting to the clit is less of an archeological dig. Since that time, I have been fixated on my pubic hair's removal.)

But the first time I saw Fred, I still had pubes and Annie was still capable of getting me to do pretty much anything.

"He wants to pluck your pubes," she'd told me. "But

don't worry because he's a really nice guy and he pays well. Plus, I'll do the session with you."

*He's a really nice guy* and he *pays well* was usually all the convincing I needed. Even if he wasn't a nice guy, "pays well" often did the trick.

We met Fred at Avalon where he requested Annie and I dress as Catholic schoolgirls. Annie had warned me that Catholic schoolgirls were another of his fetishes and that he would reference our Catholicism *ad nauseum* throughout the session. This didn't bother me, but the thought of Fred plucking my pubes did. Knowing the pain associated with simply tweezing my eyebrows, I cringed at the thought.

Fred, who was a large, goofy man in coke-bottle-glasses, started out by stripping naked and lying down on the leather bed whereupon he requested we massage him. I massaged his upper body while Annie "worked on" his lower region. As I massaged his chest, he asked, "Don't I have a nice clean body?"

"Yes, Master," I said.

"We're gonna clean up that Catholic bush of yours," he added.

"Yes, Master."

Fred, who was getting so excited that it appeared he might climax before even plucking one hair, then asked to take a break and watch Annie and I play with each other. Annie had brought along an impressive array of dildos, which we used to fuck each other in every conceivable fashion while Fred commented on our filthy, Catholic behavior. Finally, he suggested I eat Annie's pussy. She spread her legs and I worked my tongue across her clit, eventually thrusting my tongue inside of her.

"Oooooh, Master," Annie moaned, "She's fucking me with her tongue!"

"If you suck cock as well as you eat pussy, I'm going to be very impressed," Fred said. I hadn't expected to be sucking anybody's cock that day, but given I'd already sucked quite a bit of cock for money, I didn't argue.

He lay down on the bed and I started to suck him off as Annie played with his balls. We did this until he could no longer hold off on exploring his favorite fetish—pubic hairdressing.

"We're going to clean you up now," he said to me, "We're going to make you look even prettier."

The creepy factor had reached a fever pitch as I lay back and prepared for the worst. Frightened, I looked over at Annie who stood behind the hairdresser. Rather than being concerned, she was giggling hysterically.

"Annie's going to help me," Fred added.

"Oh yes, Master!" she agreed happily.

That's when Fred grabbed a couple of strands of my pubes and attempted to yank them out with his bare hands. This is no easy task, as anyone who's ever paid good money to have his or her pubes waxed will tell you. Fred attempted to "style" my hair for a good ten minutes but probably only managed to extract about three strands. The pain was not what I had expected. It hurt about as much as tweezing one's brows though I let out exaggerated yelps for effect. Fred was so caught up in the excitement of the moment that it hardly mattered to him. Meanwhile, Annie only pretended to help. Once or twice, she openly laughed and pronounced, "I got one, Master!"

Finally, Fred *had* to come. He requested I straddle his face and satisfy myself on top of him while he pleasured himself. The situation was so bizarre that I knew I would never achieve orgasm though I did my best to fake it. I also knew that the close proximity of my bush to Fred's bespectacled face would soon bring him to climax and the session would end. Meanwhile, Annie twisted Fred's nipples and sucked on them (yet another of his fetishes!) I closed my eyes and listened to Fred's frenzied moaning until he eventually achieved his hard-fought orgasm.

Carefully, I climbed off of him, helped him clean up then slipped my panties back over my still-intact Catholic bush.

# Chapter 19

## *One Year*

I saw Fred a couple more times until I eventually bid adieu to my bush forever. I didn't mind seeing him. In fact, when I think back on sessions with Fred, it seems Annie did a great service by lovingly providing him with the means to satisfy a very strange fetish.

His commentary was sometimes creepy but it was also hilarious at times. I placed Fred on the likeable end of the spectrum along with a few others, mostly rope bondage enthusiasts. I'm not saying all rope bondage enthusiasts are awesome, but the few I saw were decent. You just had to be careful with them, so they didn't tie the rope too tight or leave you in the same position for too long. Clarissa gave me specific advice when I started.

"Any tingling and you say your safe word," she told me since she didn't want anyone stroking out and dying mid-session.

My favorite of the bondage fetishists was Terrence. He was fairly attractive, young and generous, three rarities at the dungeon. I don't know what kind of Boy Scout troop he'd belonged to as a child, but he could tie a knot better than anyone I've known before or since. He was from the West Coast and when he came to town on business, he'd see me almost every day. We first met at The Inferno, but I soon trusted him enough to see him at Avalon. Eventually we scrapped the dungeons altogether and started meeting in his suite at The Four Seasons, which was great since I was welcome to the contents of his mini fridge.

The best thing about Terrence was that a*ll he did was tie me up.* He never even got naked and we were *in a hotel room!* He would just tie me up and tie me down, take a few steps back and check out his work before moving me into a new position. It was so asexual he might as well have been making model airplanes.

On the loathsome end of the spectrum there were quite a few. Chief among them was Sheldon, a banker with hairy man-boobs and martini halitosis who tried to shove his cock down my throat any time he put a blindfold over my eyes. There were days when I smoked cigarettes and did shots of whiskey just to get the taste of him out of my mouth. He used to call me "a dirty little imp" and he always tried to go over the hour. He'd order me to crawl around on my hands and knees and once even made me lick a trashcan. What he didn't know is that I preferred licking the trashcan to licking him. The trashcan was cleaner than he was.

After every miserable session I did with Sheldon, he always said the same thing—"I can tell you came." I'm not sure what gave him this impression since I never did anything to hide my misery. In the end, I think Sheldon deluded himself into believing that I liked being there. In fact, I think plenty of men did. It made them feel better about paying to see me. But I had long since realized that even though part of me was a true submissive, even though part of me wanted to be spanked, flogged and slapped, no part of me wanted to be a slave. Despite this, after a year of sessions, that's what I felt like.

A year was longer than I'd planned on working at the dungeon. A year was longer than I'd worked *anywhere.* They say time flies when you're having fun but time also flies when you're miserable and drinking yourself into a stupor to forget your misery. Somehow, all the Freds, Sheldons, Williams, Petes and bishops blurred together and made me forget I had a "plan." The plan was to work on my art, save a little and try to get a more ordinary (or at least a clothed) job as I did. But I've never been good at planning. About the only things I've ever successfully planned are outfits. Other than that, there is no trajectory for my life. I am too in the moment.

"You work really hard not to be bored," Kyle once said to me, "And that's not always good."

## Chapter 20

## We're Going to Take Your Pain Away

Maybe it was fear of being bored rather than fear of going broke that kept me working at The Inferno and at Annie's. Whatever the reason, after a year, I wanted to move on, yet I felt stuck. Several clients now had my phone number and each time they called I picked up, thinking *easy money.*

Of course it wasn't easy, but it got to be all I knew. The more I looked at the Help Wanted ads, the more despondent and desperate I became. I felt trapped.

*I don't have the balls to kill myself,* I wrote in a journal, *so instead I'm killing my soul.* I tried to blot out awareness by going on nightly benders with Kyle, Tommy, Jake and sometimes, Dylan. But when I fell asleep at night, everything I felt, all the sorrow and fear, was reflected in vivid dreams. The usual cast of characters frequently analyzed these astral adventures over drinks at Barramundi. It seemed like an excellent alternative to therapy.

In one dream I was at an orgy and I had a huge clamp on my lip. It was one of those clamps you use to hold down wood while you saw it. The clamp was so heavy that my bottom lip was hanging below my chin and my left eye was starting to fall out. Even in sleep, I could feel that it was my left eye. I wondered, in my dream, if this dream was a result of having worn nipple clamps so often at the dungeon. My left eye was falling out and I knew my right eye was next. *I am becoming blind,* I thought and then I woke up relieved that I still had eyes.

"I think your eye represents your penis here," Jake said over a pint of Pilsner.

"Jake, I don't have a penis."

"But you have a large mental phallus."

In another dream, I was in a theater searching for a floppy disc that contained some valuable writing of mine, but it was dark and disorganized in the theater. I thought I might have left the disc under a mouse pad so I'd see a mouse pad and lift it up only to find a pair of handcuffs. Torture devices seemed to be everywhere and I was crying, saying, "Where's my writing? I spent months working on it." Suddenly, Annie appeared and she promised to help me look for it, but she didn't. I was tearing the place apart and then Sheldon materialized in the theater. Even in my dream, I could smell him and it made me feel sick. He grabbed me and dragged me out into a film noir looking alley. He stripped naked and I knew he was about to rape me. Then, the weirdest thing happened—my mother appeared in the alley. "Do you want a cup of tea?" she asked. At that point, I woke up, saved by my mother and her tea.

In another dream, I was locked in a bank and outside a hurricane and tornados were raging, so perhaps I was only locked in the bank out of fear of leaving. Surrounding me were several new-age-y types.

They asked me, "Alice, have you done your healing exercises?"

And I said, "No, what are those?" So they offered to show me.

Two muscular gay men and a stoic dyke lay me down, flat upon my back on what looked like a sacrificial altar. First the dyke began to massage my feet. Then the two gay men joined in. Soon they were massaging my whole body. They said to me, "Remember your life."

And I responded, "I have no memories."

"Then how do you know you lived?"

I pondered this and the dyke said, "We're going to take your pain away."

Their hands were all over me, and it felt like they were massaging something other than my flesh, like they were getting under my skin. I started to feel like I was having a bad acid trip and the more they massaged me, the more my terror grew. My body convulsed and I started screaming. A second later, I woke up terrified.

I couldn't shake the dream from my memory. It had been so vivid, I felt like I'd been there, in the bank, on the altar, getting a massage.

"I know what it means! I know what it means!" Jake announced.

He thought that being locked in a bank represented selling out and that I started to freak out because I'm afraid of losing my artistic freedom.

"But why a dyke and why two queens?" I asked.

"Because everyone in Hollywood is gay. Duh."

"I think it means you want a massage," Kyle said.

Kyle wasn't too far off. I *did* want a massage, one so deep it would take my pain away. At age 24, my body felt arthritic and my soul felt worse.

## Chapter 21

## *White Cotton Panties*

My social life at the time revolved mostly around going to art openings and open mikes. The art openings served free wine and the open mikes were BYOB so both provided entertainment at a low price.

My open mike was a monthly all-inclusive affair held at a rundown space called The Bunny Theater where the audience sat on uncomfortable folding chairs that a bookstore had donated to the space. In the winter, the audience complained about the cold and in the summer, they complained about the heat since The Bunny had neither adequate heating nor cooling systems. But it was a space nonetheless, one where you could hang out, drink beer, smoke weed, exchange ideas and be a freewheeling bohemian in a city that was getting more expensive by the day.

"It's like there's a forty-dollar fee just for leaving your apartment," Tommy complained. He'd recently quit temping at the Dark Tower of Mordor and was trying to survive solely on freelance writing, which meant his days usually started with rejection letters. These, he sometimes read at the open mike.

"Rejection is no big deal," I tried to reassure him. "It's

just a terrible person deeming everything you've poured your heart and soul into worthless."

"Thank you, Alice. I feel much better."

Secretly, I envied Tommy for having the nuts to try freelancing. He would sit in the bookstore for hours, going through magazine mastheads and writing down the names of editors who he would then query.

"The reason I'm doing this," he told me, "Is because every day that I don't have to sit in an office or answer to the Man brings me unending joy."

Because Tommy and I vowed to stay "just friends" he occasionally brought other women to my open mike and I sometimes went home with other men, usually Stu. I never felt jealous of Tommy. I liked him so much, I was happy whenever he got laid. Sometimes we went home together but often we were too bombed to get it on.

"You can go to sleep, Alice," he'd assure me. "I won't deadhorse you or nothing. We'll just do some mean cuddlin'."

Other times we got undressed and simply explored each other's naked bodies, but there was no sex involved. We talked ten times more than we fucked. Putting sentences together was like sex for us. We certainly put more energy into it than anything else. In the morning when we were too tired to talk, *then* we'd get it on. He'd get down on his knees at the foot of my bed, pull me to him, pin my arms down and lick my cunt until I came in his mouth. This would invariably give him a throbbing boner whereupon I'd wrap my legs around him and we'd fuck like crazy. He would flip me over, pull my hair and fuck me from behind until he came.

Our resolution phase would then last for approximately 1 minute whereupon we'd start talking again, passionately and incessantly, until dusk.

Sometimes we'd continue the party, heading straight to a nearby restaurant for a six-dollar all-you-can-drink brunch with Jake and occasionally, Dylan who lived close by. I'd seen less of her at The Inferno since she'd drastically cut her hours in order to start stripping at The Paradise Club in Times Square. She preferred dancing to Domming, but hated the fact that the club managers asked her to wear a cheesy blonde wig for fear her Crayola red locks might scare away patrons.

While giving lap dances at The Paradise, she met a kid named Bradley who became a regular of hers in the lap dance room. I say "kid" because he wasn't much older than us. He was, at the most, maybe thirty. Bradley liked Dylan so much he wanted to see her privately, without the ridiculous wig and six-inch heels.

After a few weeks of him begging, she agreed to meet him outside of work on the condition he pay her two hundred and fifty bucks and send a driver to take her to the mansion in Riverdale where he lived. It was a historic, stone labyrinth of a house, which he and his sister had inherited. Since the sister was off studying in Europe, Bradley now had the run of the place. He was one of those kids you think only exists on WB TV shows—unemployed and horny with a trust fund that could feed a third world country.

Dylan later told me it had been an easy two hundred and fifty bucks. She drank his wine, sat in his hot tub, swam in his pool then gave him a massage before jerking him off and going home. Their arrangement became monthly, sometimes bimonthly and over the course of time, Dylan got to know Bradley. She discovered one of his biggest turn-ons was schoolgirl types. She told him about me and he suggested she bring me along for their next session.

A mansion with a pool and wine cellar seemed a hell of a lot more relaxing than the dungeon. I agreed to do it and that Friday night, a driver picked Dylan and me up from a diner on 23rd Street.

Bradley asked us to dress conservatively so as not to arouse the suspicions of his gossipy neighbors even though it was dark out and his house was nestled all the way in the woods, with the closest neighbor being probably five miles away. We drank, smoked and talked astrology and Witchcraft as the car made the winding 45-minute trek up the Hudson Parkway. Dylan was an out-of-the-broom-closet Wiccan who'd been studying Witchcraft and doing spells since her early teens. I had recently read a copy of Aleister Crowley's *Diary of a Drug Fiend* mostly because I tended to only read books involving sex, drugs and rock 'n' roll at the time. I fell in love with it and went on to maniacally read everything Crowley had ever written. This led me to a discovery of Wicca. I'd never been a big fan of religion, but I liked Wicca namely because it respects both the Earth and women, two things that get shat on far too often. I also liked that it resurrected the Gods and Goddesses I knew from studying art. So rather than being forced into worshipping one God who's perfect and has flowing white hair and white skin and is basically milquetoast, you got to choose from a motley group of messed-up, fascinating Gods and Goddesses. Even the seemingly perfect ones were flawed. Aphrodite was beauty incarnate but she was still jealous, vain and born from the sea foam created when Cronus lopped off Uranus's testicles and threw them into the ocean. Pan had a bevy of nymphs but he was still a lonely, misunderstood, goat-legged musician. The Old Gods were crazy, lonely, jealous and bored, just like us.

Dylan was a wellspring of information on Gods, Goddesses and generally, all things magickal. She was also studying astrology and had recently done my chart in exchange for a drawing.

"So you still haven't told me what the stars have in store for me," I said as we shared a bottle of cider in the back of the sedan.

"Well, for starters, you have Venus in your twelfth house."

"You said that like you're telling me I have cancer."

"It just means you'll always chase impossible love because you know what you want in every area of your life except love."

"I don't care about that. Will I ever be rich? That's a much bigger concern right now."

"You'll be incredibly successful and yes, someday you'll have money."

"Do you know when?"

"Nope. It doesn't give you specific dates."

Eventually, our astrology talk was cut short when we reached what looked like Middle Earth and Bradley's house.

He greeted us in the driveway, paid the driver and quickly smuggled us inside lest anyone see us. He was short and stocky with reddish brown hair and dimples.

He offered us wine and after making some small talk, suggested we all go for a swim. I'd brought along a bikini but realized I wouldn't be using it when Dylan stripped naked and dove in the pool. I did the same and soon we were all swimming together naked. After a couple more glasses of wine we moved to the hot tub where we smoked weed and talked. Bradley seemed lonely and despite his wealth, I didn't envy him.

Pretty soon things in the hot tub got touchy feely and he suggested we move into the bedroom where Dylan and I would "put on a show." Like any theatrical production, costumes were required. Dylan would wear sleazy black lingerie and I would wear my schoolgirl uniform, which I was getting real tired of.

Dylan would play the aggressor and start groping me. Eventually clothes would come off and Dylan would strap on a dildo and fuck my brains out in every conceivable manner.

Having strapped one on myself, I know the only real kick you can get out of fucking someone with a piece of plastic is psychological. I felt bad that Dylan would have to do all the work and reap none of the sensory rewards, but Bradley wanted to watch "the vamp" corrupting "the schoolgirl." Funny, since I was now *more* corrupt than Dylan whose boundaries included not fucking her clients.

We got down to business with Dylan kissing and undressing me until all I wore were knee socks and my pleated miniskirt. I returned the favor, unhooking her bra to reveal her enormous breasts, which I licked and sucked. We were both getting turned on, both of us dripping wet and forgetting about Bradley's presence even though he was sitting mere inches from us, stroking his cock. When Dylan lifted my skirt and began giving me head, I felt like we were acting out someone's Penthouse Forum letter.

"Fuck me," I whispered in her ear and sure enough, she whipped out her dildo, strapped it on and fucked me. When she fucked me from behind I played with myself until I came.

I had fully expected Bradley to blow his load watching this, but he hadn't.

"I take a long time," he said, suggesting we "help him out."

Dylan knew what this meant. Reaching for an enormous bottle of moisturizer that sat by the bed, she pumped some out, lubed him up and stroked his cock while he instructed me to masturbate in front of him. I was tired from the wine, the weed and the fucking but was in no position to argue. Spreading my legs, I put on another show until he came.

Dylan and I both went home two hundred and fifty dollars richer, which wasn't much considering the show we put on. However, we figured we'd had about one hundred dollars worth of wine and weed, which more than made up for it.

We did a few more sessions with Bradley until eventually he asked if I would be comfortable seeing him alone. At that point, very little made me uncomfortable so I agreed to it. However, he then offered to pick me up, which *did* make me uncomfortable. My clients could have everything above 14th Street and beyond but the Lower East Side was *my* territory. I didn't like the idea of it being invaded.

To make matters worse, he pulled up in front of my building in a ridiculous convertible, the kind where the doors open up like batwings. He would have been less conspicuous pulling up in a tank. For the first time in my life (okay, maybe the second), I felt like a real call girl.

When we finally got to his place, he offered me a beer and a cigarette. I downed the beer but somehow refused the cig. Although we'd been chatting the whole way there, the sound of my voice echoing in the house now made me self-conscious. Finally he asked, "Do you want to sit in the Jacuzzi?" I nodded my head and followed him.

It wasn't long before getting naked and kissing in the Jacuzzi led to drying off and reclining on the nearby chaise lounges.

"I'm not sure how far you want to go," he said. "But, I have these just in case." He held out a pack of Trojans. "I don't want to put any pressure on you. You're the boss, okay?"

"I'm willing to go as far as you want," I said, unwrapping my towel and reclining further.

He lay next to me and we kissed. My hands wandered down to his crotch, and his hands were everywhere. Soon he was on top of me and his fingers were deep inside of me. I ran my tongue up and down his chest and then down to his lower stomach. He moved up and straddled my face, and I kissed his shaft and tickled the tip of his penis with my tongue, until I took him all the way in my mouth.

Soon he reached for a condom, slipped it on and thrust into me hard. We then proceeded to fuck for over an hour, moving from the poolside to the bedroom to a guest bedroom just for the hell of it. Eventually, he asked me to masturbate while he watched and jerked himself off. We lay together for a moment before heading downstairs. I took the cigarette he'd offered earlier and smoked while collecting the clothes I'd left by the pool.

As I dressed, he picked up my white cotton panties and said, "You know how to make my fantasies come true."

"Thanks," I lied.

The session hadn't been awful. In fact, I'd had an orgasm. But I was feeling very much like I'd outgrown my white cotton panties along with the idea of being someone else's fantasy. I just wanted to be real, to be back with my friends on the Lower East Side who knew my flaws but loved me anyway. The fact that Bradley knew my name was really Alice, and not June, hardly mattered. He'd just fucked June, a façade I'd about perfected.

## Chapter 22

## Sacrifice

Bradley became a regular. Sometimes I saw him out in Riverdale and sometimes he rented hotel rooms where we'd order room service and get drunk on champagne. Sessions with him were physically pleasurable though still painful in that I was selling my ass and not my art. Even so, they were ten times better than sessions with Lord H. Hours spent with him were becoming unendurable physically and mentally.

Lord H started bringing me presents, things I didn't want. First he gave me an expensive hairbrush he'd originally used to abuse my ass. Then he gave me a wool schoolgirl getup similar to the ones in Annie's closet. Finally, he gave me a silver ring he'd gotten in Ireland. It was actually three skinny band rings in one, attached at the center. The bands moved up and down and I fidgeted with them especially during sessions. Because the ring didn't leave a green mark on my finger, I figured it must be worth something. I used the brush and wore the ring constantly either because I really was his slave or because I wanted to remind myself of how badly I wanted freedom.

I didn't want to become like Annie who was completely financially dependent on him. My first impression of Annie had been that she was strong, fearless and alive, but now I saw that he was killing her. During one session, she'd been on her period and he insisted on going down on her. He *wanted* to taste her blood. His grey beard was covered in blood as he lifted his head from between her legs. It looked like he'd just slaughtered and eaten an animal. And as Annie writhed around, pretending to come, all I saw was a sacrificial animal. And next to the sacrifice, all I saw was a vampire.

Walking home from that session, I thought about the conversation I'd had with Kyle more than a year earlier when he'd told me he didn't want me to lose my innocence. I'd told him there were almost as many definitions for innocence as there were for love, but I wasn't sure. A former vocab nerd, I often talked out my ass about the meaning of words without checking. I needed to check, to be sure I still had a little of what I considered innocence. At home I pulled out my dictionary and turned to "innocence." There were 8 definitions.

*in·no·cence n:*
*1. the state of not being guilty of a crime or offense*
*2. the state of being permitted by law*
*3. harmlessness in intention*
*4. freedom from sin or evil*
*5. a lack of experience of the world, especially when this results in a failure to recognize the harmful intentions of other people*

*6. ignorance of the serious consequences of something such as an act or remark*
*7. sexual inexperience*
*8. See blue-eyed Mary*

Scanning the list, my first thought was, *what the fuck is a blue-eyed Mary?* I then "saw" blue-eyed Mary and discovered it was a North American plant of the snapdragon family that has blue and white flowers. That settled I turned back to innocence. Botany aside, innocence, it seemed fell into three categories—legal, sexual and moral. In a court of law, I would be considered guilty of prostitution. And sexually, I obviously was not innocent. In fact, Encarta would almost need a new category for me the way I was going. But in terms of morality, I was still doing okay. *Morally* I didn't think prostitution was a crime and morally I had no intention of harming anyone. I hadn't been raised on religion but I had read all the great Greek plays and if they taught me anything it was that morals, divine law and respect for every living being mattered more than crap like chastity and legal minutiae. Be able to live with yourself and sleep at night. That's it.

But however good it might have felt to realize that I still retained the only innocence that mattered, something about the fourth definition made my arm hairs stand on end. *Freedom from sin or evil.*

I thought of the blood on the bishop's beard and the coldness in his eyes. He was a man who preached about sin and evil—two words that make me uncomfortable—two words

I'd replace with "immoral" and "hypocritical." And the bishop was a hypocrite. He would tell others that they'd be denied God's grace for the very acts he performed privately. Instinctively, I kept my distance from him. Even if physically, I allowed him to penetrate every part of my body, I never revealed my thoughts to him. He never knew I was a painter and writer. He never knew I was even vaguely intelligent and he never saw an emotional state coming from me that was anything more than pure agony.

I would say all the things Lord H wanted to hear like "Yes, Lord, I'll bleed for you!" And, "Of course you can beat me till I bleed." But in reality, I would never let that man touch or taste my blood. I was still just a "toy" to him and Annie and I didn't want it to go further than that. I wanted to remain as free from his hypocrisy as possible. Of course, each time I took his money I became a little less so. For all my talk of Greek plays and morals, I was no Antigone.

Annie and I weren't really close either despite constantly having sex with each other. For starters, her girlfriend, Luna, had grown extremely jealous of me (probably because of the aforementioned sex) and anytime Annie wasn't in session, she was with Luna who scared the bejesus out of me. The only time Annie and I got to talk was before clients arrived. One day, before William arrived, she told me she'd seen Lord H the day before, and that she'd told him he was getting too heavy. Telling him, she said, just made him worse. When she got undressed, I noticed her ass was black and blue. She also had cigarette burns up and down her arms and I asked her if he'd given her those too.

"No. Those were for fun with Luna."

Two weeks earlier, Annie and I had done a session with H, in which he'd attempted to use a paddle so large and ominous that it was akin to a boat oar. When I saw it, I freaked out.

"No way," I said.

"Don't be a baby," was his response.

Lord H became more heavy-handed around the time he met Shannon, another slave who lived in Ireland. Shannon could apparently take an even harder session than Annie—a pain threshold incomprehensible to me. However, I came and went. I did the bare minimum and the more you take on a regular basis, the easier it is to endure—physically anyway. Psychologically, I think it becomes harder assuming you're not doing it for love. Annie saw H once a week and I only saw him once every two or three months.

The "boat oar" paddle had been part of Lord H's birthday session, an event Annie and I had been dreading ever since the previous year's "celebration" when we both received *his* birthday spanking, administered with his favorite wooden hairbrush.

He had us guess his age and for each year of his life we got one spanking, and for each year we were off we got two spankings. I remember thinking that he looked to be about my mother's age, so I guessed fifty. He was actually fifty-one, so that made for a combined total of fifty-three. Annie guessed fifty-two, so she also got fifty-three.

H's fixation with the hairbrush, Annie finally told me, dated back to his childhood, which was no surprise since childhood is when everyone gets fucked up. The great thing about being a child is that you get to discover the beautiful things like the smell of honeysuckle, but the terrible thing about childhood is you also discover the horrible things. At least when you're an adult, you already know the world is a warring, starving place where the rich man's heaven is the poor man's hell.

So if I came away from the sex industry with one tiny bit of wisdom, it's that childhood fucks everyone up in one way or another. Take for instance, Fred, the pubic-hair plucker. I later found out he grew up on a chicken farm. I imagined little Fred watching chickens in an overcrowded roost area plucking out each other's feathers in order to make more room and the horror he must have felt over their desperate act. Adults will often sexualize whatever horrors they witnessed as children in order to make them bearable.

Strangely enough, my own childhood had been somewhat idyllic. I was properly parented, educated and loved. I was the youngest so I got picked on, but not so harshly that it would have indicated "professional masochist" later in life. The only thing that ever really fucked me up was refusing to be anything but an artist.

Anyway, according to Annie, H's mother used to beat him and his little sister with a wooden hairbrush. She wouldn't stop until his sister cried. As an adult, he gets off watching women who are dressed as little girls cry while he beats them with a similar wooden hairbrush. I later wished she never told me this because it made me pity him, which was much harder than hating him. To see that behind the hypocrite there was a suffering human being was a terrible realization.

So during the second birthday session we endured with him, I suggested to Annie that we hide the hairbrush, but she pointed out there's not much use hiding one implement of torture in a room filled with canes, whips and paddles.

During the previous birthday celebration, I had a terrible hangover. My stomach felt empty and I was sweating booze. Luna, who was seething with jealousy that day, continually knocked on Annie's front door while we attempted to conduct our session. When we didn't answer the door, she began calling incessantly. Along with this debacle, and my hangover, was the terrible scratchiness of my heavy-knit schoolgirl outfit. On that day, it was driving me crazy. I wanted to peel it off and lie naked in the arms of someone warm and whole.

H said he wanted to see me cry, and when my tears started flowing, they wouldn't stop even when he wasn't beating me—tears of nervous exhaustion. By the end of the session, which took forever, because of Luna's interruptions, my face was soaked with tears. When I got home that day, I lay down on the kitchen floor, and thought, *I will never do this again.*

Jump ahead one year and there I was, doing it again, and again thinking, *I'll never do this again.*

"I just hope he's in a good mood today," Annie whispered to me as we walked into the room at Avalon we'd rented for the session. We kissed him on the cheek and wished him a happy birthday.

"So, you're fifty-two today," Annie said, as if to eliminate the birthday spanking game.

"You remembered," he said, feigning surprise.

He'd requested I wear my usual plaid schoolgirl outfit, but for some reason he'd asked Annie to wear overalls and a long brown wig that looked like my hair. We resembled a prissy schoolgirl and a tomboy, sort of a *Facts of Life* Blair/Jo fantasy.

"I brought you both a new toy," he added, pulling a massive, double-ended dildo out of his bag of tricks. It was frighteningly large, but less scary than the brush.

He warmed us up with his usual, ultra-hard spanking. He always spanked Annie and me harder than anyone else ever did, lifting his hand all the way in the air and bringing it down with all his strength. He then took a break and watched while Annie and I spanked each other.

Afterward, he ordered me to lift up my skirt, and pull down my cotton underpants so he could take a close-up Polaroid picture of my already bright red ass. I never let him photograph my face, but I didn't mind when he took pictures of my ass or pussy. The photo session time cut into the torture time.

After doling out more corporal punishment, we were stripped naked and told to lie down spread-eagle on the leather bed. He then put a condom on each end of the dildo and thrust one end of it inside of me. Annie opened her legs, and he thrust the other end inside of her. He said he wanted to see "how much" we could fit inside of us, so we slowly thrust toward each other. He put one hand on the dildo and thrust it in and out of us, roughly (as he did everything.) With his other hand, he worked us over with Annie's vibrator.

He then lay the vibrator down and circled the bed, massaging our breasts. He bent over me and told me to lick his balls. He walked over to Annie, and she did the same. He again took out his Polaroid and snapped a couple of pictures of our pussies, which were connected by the shared dildo.

He finally took the dildo out, and told us to get ready for our birthday spanking. The anticipation of such an event is almost as bad as the event itself.

I bent over his lap, and he gave me ten with the wooden hairbrush. At ten I leapt out of his grasp. It was Annie's turn. I watched as he gave her ten and she struggled. He pulled me back over his lap and gave me ten more. I was soon in tears, not from emotional pain or heartache, but simply from pain. He gave us each fifty whacks, telling us he would save the last two for later.

He wanted to take more pictures, and asked us if we had to pee since he *really* wanted to photograph us pissing. I had been drinking water all day, and desperately had to pee, but peeing in front of him, in front of his camera seemed to be crossing a line even if he was only going to document my crotch. But again, peeing seemed a lot more enjoyable than torture.

He laid out "wee-wee pads" and told us to pee directly on them. Annie did this without hesitation, and he took some close-ups of the stream of urine shooting out of her pussy. I had a hard time peeing and only got a little stream going.

However, we all took note of the fact that I'd taken a ton of vitamins because my urine was an unearthly, fluorescent yellow.

We cleaned ourselves off with baby wipes and paper towels. I had taken my watch off, but I had a feeling that the session was drawing to an end.

H told me to lie down on the bed and "show Annie some affection." We tended to end many sessions this way so I knew what he meant. I got on all fours, on top of Annie, and planted my face in her crotch. She moaned as he unwrapped a condom. He knelt behind me and thrust his cock inside my pussy.

He pumped in and out of me, whispering, "Do you want to take the hairbrush? Do you want your ass to bleed?"

"Yes, Sir."

The thrusting got harder as I felt the ungodly stinging of the hairbrush on my ass. His breathing grew heavier as tears ran down my face. He grunted and then let out one long moan that signaled the end of my torture.

He climbed off of me, and gave Annie and me each a kiss on the lips. And despite the fact that he'd just come, he wasn't finished. He told us to bend over his knee for our final spanking, and we each took one more with the hairbrush.

I quickly put on my clothes and wondered if I'd see him again on his next birthday. The session seemed easier than the year before and I thought *maybe I'm getting used to it.* Maybe I had resigned myself to the sex industry.

My body was so sore I took a painkiller to fall asleep. When I finally dozed off, I dreamt that I was in some sort of gymnasium. There were a bunch of men there, all wearing black Speedos. They were taking hot showers because they were freezing cold and they were actually *crying* because they were so cold. They didn't say this, but in dreams you sometimes "just know" things and in this dream, I knew they were crying because they were so cold. Kyle appeared and we watched the crying men together. I turned to him and asked, "Have you ever been so cold you cried?"

And he said, "Everyone has."

# Chapter 23

## *You Make Me Feel Like a Pervert*

My days at The Inferno had been numbered ever since discovering I could make ten times more money being a freelance slave. I'd also grown concerned over various receptionists at The Inferno forgetting to knock lightly on the door when my sessions ended. This was protocol for all sessions and was especially important for sub sessions since often I was tied up when the hour tolled and there was no way I could check the time. Usually, I tried to time sessions by the length of the CD playing, but some clients preferred quiet. Therefore, I sometimes worked for an hour and a half and only got paid for an hour.

Not only that, I was physically and emotionally exhausted from doing sub work. Some nights I lay in the bathtub and looked at the bruises on my legs and felt so broken I wanted to sink or disappear or bleed everything out of me till I was air. I thought about a quote from one of my favorite movies, Fellini's *La Dolce Vita*. A poet character says, "The only thing that matters is to burn." This is true for artists. If you are an artist, that burning also known as passion is what gets you out of bed in the morning. Mine was fading fast.

One night at the bar with Tommy after he'd had a million

pints and a little weed, he said, "You are like that girl with garlands and flowers that's always following the circus."

"But, I'm morbidly depressed."

I was tired of following the circus—the acrobats ready to fall, the crying clowns and the dancing, tortured animals—the circus was much sadder than advertised.

"But you've got joie de vivre," he slurred.

"Not for long."

As we were having this very conversation, a bespectacled hipster entered the back room holding up a copy of Sartre's *Existentialism and Human Emotions*.

"Does this belong to you?" he asked innocently.

"We *are* existentialism and human emotions," I said.

He gave me the book and Tommy and I laughed so hard we cried.

The next day I had a revelation; the first of many. I had to leave the sex industry before it extinguished the part of me that was the girl with garlands and flowers, the girl one of my professors had nicknamed "Sunbeam" because he said I shone so brightly.

I went into The Inferno a few hours later and announced my "retirement." No need for two weeks notice since I wouldn't be asking for references. I walked to my locker, hastily packed up my things and walked out, telling myself I was through. I would pick up a copy of the *New York Times* that day and get to work looking for a real job. I would take my body back and become a normal, functioning member of society.

A week later, The Inferno had a new sub—a friend of

Dylan's who I heard could take a much heavier session than me. Unfortunately, after only two weeks on the job, she too became unemployed when a client broke two of her ribs during a session. When I caught wind of this, I promised myself I would never do it again.

I walked all over the city, handing out phony résumés wherein Tommy was a CEO and I had been his personal assistant. He even changed his outgoing message to reflect this lest anyone should call. Eventually I landed a job at a French boutique in SoHo. The Man was, in this case, a lady with dyed black hair who wore too much foundation. She wanted me to literally attack customers and force the store's heinous, overpriced clothes on them. I was terrible at it, too shy to sell anything. After three days there, when the boss sent me on my break in the middle of a monsoon, I decided to get wet and not return. I walked without an umbrella to Kyle's doorstep. He let me up and we shared a beer, toasting my unemployment.

I continued looking for work, handing out résumés and scanning the paper, but the *Times* was full of job listings *for people with skills*. And I was a painter and writer with *no skills*. I went to Kmart, and they weren't even hiring. I went to millions of temp agencies, but no one hired me. It's like they could smell the freak in me.

I felt cast out of this world. The only industry that accepted me was the sex industry, and even then, only the very fringes of the sex industry. So, a month later, I ran out of money and found myself at yet another dungeon where I knew they would hire me right away. Initially, I had been so proud when I walked out of The Inferno. But, here I was, traipsing into the office of yet another exploiter in midtown, asking for a job.

The proprietor, a hard-looking, red-lipped, shriveled woman with a bob-hairdo, looked me over and said, "You make me feel like a pervert and that's gonna make you a lot of money."

She was pleased that I had worked at The Inferno even though I explained that it was a stinking hellhole. She was proud of her place, although it was a dump. There were only two small rooms, both of which were scantily equipped and furnished. There was no Versailles Room, no gilded rococo mirrors, no rotating walls, no fluffy powder blue carpets, no client waiting room or penis-shaped door handles.

About the only thing this nameless joint shared with The Inferno was the smell of Lysol and cum, but at no less than eighty-five bucks an hour, and less than zero bucks in my bank account, I wasn't about to open my mouth and bitch about the crummy interior décor.

The hard woman with the bob hairdo asked me if I could start that night and went over the terms and rules of her space. "There's no sex, you know," she told me, "But, if somebody offers you enough for a blowjob, or something, it's up to you."

I was shocked. At The Inferno everyone sucked cock and fucked, but no one ever admitted it publicly. No one ever made mention of it, or even suggested that there was any leniency regarding the rules whatsoever. It was refreshing to be in an environment, where the proprietor was at least honest about what really goes on. I always despised the euphemisms that were so rampant at The Inferno, like the use of the term "hand-release" when what they really meant was hand-job. This place was gross, but at least it was honest.

I went home, napped and came back, carrying a little bag of lingerie and a schoolgirl uniform. The waiting room was tiny, and packed with four bitchy girls who hated me on sight. As long as I could get the receptionist to like me, that was the important part. If the receptionist hated you, you could forget about ever making a dime. She would withhold your description from any prospective clients, thus causing your sadomasochistic endeavor to go belly up.

The receptionist seemed impressed when I told her I could take a "heavy" session. I put my little bag in the waiting room and popped open a book. I then tried to make conversation with my new coworkers, but found it difficult. Two of them were obviously junkies and one was a speed-freak who was rapidly making beaded bracelets. The other was a fat brunette Mistress who made Chesty Morgan look like an A-cup. A bad TV miniseries about a serial killer was on, but nobody watched it. Eventually, the speed-freak warmed up to me and asked if I wanted to make a bracelet. I felt like the new kid in school who had just been befriended by the biggest outcast in the school. She told me that she was a Dom as was the well-endowed brunette. The junkies, she told me, were "switchables."

The receptionist knocked. A particularly heavy client had arrived. He was a regular, interested in seeing "the new girl."

"Do you want to talk to him?" the receptionist asked me.

"Sure," I said, throwing on my heels and following her to one of the two small rooms.

Perhaps it was the fact that I'd just been watching a miniseries about a serial killer, but when I walked in the room, that's the vibe I got. He had already removed his clothes, and was sitting there in ripped, dirty tighty-whities. He had a long white beard like a maniacal hillbilly, and a Manson-esque quality to his stare.

I introduced myself and asked, "What are you into?"

"Have you ever been beaten?" he answered.

I left the room. Desperate as I was, the sound of his voice made my arm hairs stand on end. I went back to the waiting room and sat down.

"He's all yours," the receptionist said to one of the junkies, a tall redhead. She moped out of the room.

The speed freak whispered in my ear, "That was a smart decision. She won't sit for a week."

The brunette turned up the TV, but we could still hear the sound of the maniac beating her. I could hear her guttural crying. I tried to make a bracelet but it was impossible. Eventually, the buzzer rang. A new guy, into light "sensual" domination had arrived. Would I be interested? The receptionist wanted to know.

I walked into the room. He was in his mid-twenties and very attractive, but not the sort of person I would date. He looked like a Marine, with a crew cut and muscular arms. From his twang, I guessed he was Southern. Just possibly, the Universe had smiled upon my weary soul.

I asked him what he was into.

"Blindfolds, spanking, face-slapping and lingerie," he said.

He didn't sound too confident and I got the feeling he'd probably never done this before. I went outside and told the receptionist I'd take it. I then went into the waiting room and changed into my black slip, thigh-highs and patent-leather pumps. I could still hear the junky whimpering and the speed freak had now almost completed what appeared to be an incredibly intricate bracelet.

I knocked lightly on the door. When my new client answered, his eyes lit up. I stood motionless in front of him.

"You look beautiful," he said.

He moved closer, reached his hands around and grabbed both of my ass cheeks like he owned them, which for all intents and purposes, he did that hour. He leaned in and kissed me on the lips, which normally I found repulsive when dealing with clients. But with "the Marine" I became quickly aroused. He thrust his tongue inside my mouth and I opened my mouth wider. He let go of my ass and lightly slapped my face. He did it a second time.

"You can do it harder," I said.

He looked both surprised and pleased and responded by slapping me harder. It stung but I was growing wetter, imagining he was doing things to me he'd only dreamed of doing with girlfriends

"Bend over the table," he said.

I bent over the table, a black leather number that could've

used some new upholstery, and thrust my ass in the air. He began to spank me, but soon stopped in order to caress my ass. His fingers eventually made their way up my slip and inside my g-string where he discovered that I was absolutely soaking wet. He rubbed my clit and I moaned, sticking my ass out further. He got the idea and slowly thrust his fingers in and out of me with one hand. With the other, he fondled my breasts. This went on until I was on the brink of orgasm, but he forestalled it by telling me to turn around and take off my slip.

I pulled the slip over my head and stood facing him in my thigh-highs, g-string and pumps. He took his shirt off, revealing a well-sculpted chest. Without any prompting, I kissed it, running my tongue across his skin and licking up beads of perspiration, which had formed in the hot little room. He pushed my head toward his crotch and I ran my tongue along the trail of hair leading toward his belt buckle. His hard-on pressed against my hands as I ran them along the surface of his jeans. Finally, he undid his belt and yanked down his pants followed by his briefs whereupon a gorgeous erection greeted me. After having seen so many shrunken, dysfunctional cocks at The Inferno, it was nice to see a fine, functioning piece of machinery. He stroked himself and I was so aroused that I plunged my right hand inside my g-string and stroked myself. With my left hand, I then began stroking his cock for him. I couldn't believe it! I'd only been at the new place for a few hours and already I'd ignored all of the rules. Eventually I dropped to my knees and his cock made its way into my mouth. As

I sucked him off, I stroked myself until I came. He then pulled his cock out of my mouth and beat off until he came on my tits.

We'd barely spoken and even after we were both sweaty and satisfied there wasn't much to say except, "Baby Wipes?" After we'd cleaned ourselves off and collected ourselves, he asked, "That was amazing. Are you here all the time?"

"Now I am."

He gave me a fifty-dollar tip, which along with the eighty-five from the receptionist made the evening quite profitable. I said goodbye and returned to the waiting room where I got dirty looks from everyone. The junky was back from her session with the maniac. Her eyes were swollen and her face was tearstained. She was in her own world, standing up and holding onto the side of the table. The speed freak was still beading and no one was speaking to each other. The "Marine" or whatever he was had been a delight but the nameless dungeon was the most miserable place in the universe, in heaven or hell, a circle lower than The Inferno.

## Chapter 24

## *Sleeping Beauty*

Despite being freaked out by the nameless dungeon's sad, drug-addled staff and their regular maniacal client, I returned two days later. In the waiting room I read a book on feral children, and tried to ignore the fact that no one there was speaking to me. After an hour, a client arrived. The receptionist who had already taken a liking to me, given I was actually conscious, offered me the session. She told me his name was "Sam" and he was a regular, into role-play and "smothering."

I walked into the client waiting room and found a tiny Hasidic man. He looked embarrassed and didn't make eye contact when we spoke.

"What do you want to do?" I asked.

"I want you to pretend like you're asleep, and that I come into the room and begin to undress you. You wake up while I'm undressing you and you get angry. You try to fight me, but I hold you down. At that point, you submit and I finish undressing you. I then smother you."

Since he looked to be about 120 pounds soaking wet, the thought of him smothering me was not intimidating.

I wore a pink slip, white lace-trimmed thigh-highs, a white g-string and a white lace bra, a far cry from what

I normally sleep in (either nothing at all or an oversized, filthy Washington Capitals jersey I got at age twelve.) Sam removed his many layers of clothing, stripping all the way down to his black trousers, revealing a chest that was pale and speckled with moles. He motioned for me to lie down on the couch. I lay down and stretched out in an unrealistic fashion, like a Playboy bunny posing for a photo shoot. He walked out and closed the door. Immediately, he walked back in and locked the door. His hands gently caressed the surface of my clothing.

"Aha," he said, "I'm going to undress you and you'll never even know." It was very childlike, a land of make-believe born out of his frustrated fantasies. He then pulled my slip over my head and unhooked my bra. He pressed his hands against my bare breasts and moaned. He unpeeled my stockings, but when he got to my g-string, I opened my eyes and he cowered with shame.

"What are you doing to me?" I gasped.

"I can do whatever I want to you," he asserted, pinning my hands down. I pretended to struggle while doing some terrible soap opera acting.

Finally, my g-string was on the floor and I lay there naked and cold. He unzipped his pants to reveal the outline of a small, hard cock beneath a pair of worn out briefs. He began to smother me, rubbing his crotch against my crotch. His movements were quick and afraid, as he rubbed his body all over mine and even straddled my head. He pulled his briefs down, backed up and stared at me while masturbating himself to orgasm.

A few nights later, I went to Jake's open mike where I read two stories, one about sucking off the "Marine" and one about being smothered by the Hasid.

"Wow," Kyle said, as I sat back down next to him, "You managed to give me a raging boner and a softee all within an eight-minute time frame."

"I had a little 'movement'," Tommy agreed.

Later, when the three of us went outside for a smoke, Tommy said to me, "You should take that story about the Marine, add a little extra cheese, maybe add some fucking and send it off to *mess* or *Cheri* or one of those magazines. They'd publish that shit in a heartbeat."

"I'd read it. Of course I'd have to shoplift it, but I would read it," Kyle agreed.

The thought of writing for mainstream porn had never occurred to me, but it made sense. Writers always say, "Write about what you know," and if I knew one thing, it was sex, and not just sex but male fantasy. I'd been catering to it for well over a year.

I had nothing and therefore had nothing to lose. The following day, flushed with embarrassment, I went to the local porn shop/smoke shop/bodega and stocked up. I bought *Oui, Cheri, Penthouse* and *Penthouse Variations* along with a scratch-off ticket and a granola bar. Somehow I thought the scratch-off ticket and granola bar might offset the attention I was calling to myself by purchasing a stack of porn. It didn't as every hairy eyeball in the place latched directly onto me while I fumbled through my purse for cash.

Outside, I played the scratch-off and miraculously won

twenty-five dollars, about what I had paid for the porn. I went back into the porn shop/smoke shop/bodega and collected my winnings.

I took winning scratch-off as a clear sign—I was one the right path.

When I got home, I sat in front of Jake's busted old PC he let me use and began to write. I aimed to give the world a boner and in the process, free myself from slavery.

## Chapter 25

## *What's Next?*

I was making enough cash doing sessions with Annie and her clients that I barely worked at the nameless dungeon. I figured if I spent too much time there, I too would develop a drug habit. And with Con Ed, AT&T and my landlord breathing down my neck, a drug habit was not something I could afford. The little bob-haired lady who ran the joint was happy to have me anytime I called and needed work, but I hardly ever did. Along with Annie's clients, I was still seeing Bradley, who I feared was falling for me. He once handed me a wad of cash at the end of a session and said, "I don't like to think of this arrangement as what it actually is. Please think of this as a donation or a friend giving you money because you need it." It was almost like getting a grant based on the merit of my vagina.

Meanwhile, sessions at Annie's were getting weirder by the week, especially when it came to William and Lord H. During one session with William, he insisted I pee in a cup and then drink my own piss.

"No way," I said. Drinking *my own* pee would be less humiliating than drinking *someone else's* pee, but it was just not my cup of tea. My cup of tea was tea, not urine.

"Gandhi drank his own pee," Annie insisted.

"Yeah, but Gandhi drank his own pee because he was trying to stay alive. My situation is hardly that dire."

Somehow, she convinced me to do it (as she did with everything) and moments later I was peeing in a cup then drinking it. My urine tasted salty, much like my tears. In a blind taste test, I guarantee subjects would be unable to differentiate between the two. In the end, I realized drinking my own pee was far from terrible, which is something no one should ever have to realize.

A few nights after this completely useless realization, I met up with Stu at the bar. We hadn't seen each other in a few weeks and the chemistry was cataclysmic due possibly due to the full moon coupled with our own despairing loneliness. Chemistry is the one thing you can't fake. You can pretend to like someone or even pretend to love them but chemistry is what happens when normally dormant atoms within the genitals and brain spring to life upon seeing someone. And that night in June, everything sprang to life.

I was wearing a pink and white striped tube top I'd gotten on Clinton Street for ninety-nine cents along with a pair of turquoise hot pants. Stu sat on a bar stool with his legs open and I wiggled between them, pressing my belly into his crotch. Reaching my hand between his thighs, I could feel his erection. He fiddled with my tube top.

"Did boys pull your tube top down in high school?" he asked.

"Boys ignored me in high school. Plus, no one wore tube tops in the '80s. I'm trying to make them cool again."

"Well, I like them, especially on you, though it doesn't seem to be keeping you very warm," he said referring to my eternally erect nipples. He leaned down and kissed my neck. "Let's get the fuck out of here," he finally said.

We gulped down our pints and walked back to my place in a state of crazed sexual arousal, kissing as we made our way up the stairs, he with a raging hard-on and me with soaked panties. Once we were finally inside, he picked me up and carried me into my bedroom, plopping me down on my bed, which still had a broken box spring. He unzipped his fly and grabbing a handful of my hair, pulled my head toward his cock, which was now exposed, given he was prone to going commando. I licked and kissed the tip then let it plunge into my throat. As I gave him head, I stealthily removed my hot pants and played with myself.

Eventually he pulled out of my mouth and yanked my tube top down, savagely biting into my nipples and rubbing his cock between my tiny breasts. We undressed and he reached for a condom, a red Trojan. I wrapped my legs around his shoulders and he thrust deeply inside of me, moving in and out fast and hard. When he grew tired, we flipped over and I got on top, continuing the frantic pace of our fucking until Stu announced he was about to come.

I hadn't come, but after a few pints, I sometimes didn't. Sex was the one thing I preferred doing sober. Now that I'm in my thirties I can hardly walk down the street without coming, but in those days, it wasn't so easy especially if I'd been drinking. This is why companies like L'Oréal and Oil of Olay target women in their thirties—to make them feel guilty for coming so goddamned much. Even so, orgasm has never been the goal for me, closeness has, that, and the exchange of energy. If sex is a vacation from reality, why go on a vacation just to focus on it ending?

But on that night, when the moon was full and my hot pants and tube top lay in a crumpled mess next to the bed, the vacation from reality came to a crashing halt.

Stu did come and as he did, the condom broke. I'd had my period approximately two weeks earlier and I knew immediately—I was pregnant.

"Oh fuck! Go and clean yourself out," Stu yelled at me, as if it were somehow my fault, as if my *vagina dentata* fangs had ripped the condom to shreds.

I was in something like a state of shock so I hesitated.

"Go!" he said again.

In the bathroom, I tried to "wash" his semen out of me but I knew it was too late. I'd been on top when it happened so his jizz had shot so far inside me it was practically floating in my eyeballs. Plan B wasn't available at the time so I was pretty much fucked. I didn't know much about pregnancy, but I knew one little Olympic swimmer of a sperm had raced for its life and made it to shore. I could feel it.

It sounds ridiculous but the next day my stomach was already bigger and my appetite was raging. I hadn't eaten meat in years and suddenly my body craved both meat and milk. I would've run somebody over for a turkey sandwich with cheese.

In my ignorance, I didn't realize you had to wait for a missed period to get a correct result from a pregnancy test.

(I think this technology has advanced in recent years.) So, I walked to Gem Home Store on Delancey Street and bought a test. It came back negative. Still, I knew I was pregnant. I took a few more and all of them came back negative. Finally, my "Little Red Bastard" didn't arrive on time. Little Red Bastard was a term Kyle and I had come up with to replace the more gentle euphemisms for menstruation like "Aunt Flow." Menstruation was an absolute bastard that required maintenance and supplies. I refused to call it anything pleasant. Still, getting your period was better than getting no period at all.

"I know I'm fucking preggers," I told Kyle. "I can feel it, but every test is coming back negative."

"Well, listen. Take one more. I'll buy it for you if you buy me beer."

We walked to the CVS near his apartment where we picked up a six-pack and a pregnancy test.

"Oh, look! It comes in a two-pack!" Kyle noted. "I'll take it with you."

When we got to the counter, Kyle asked the clerk, "Do you think she looks pregnant?"

He sized me up. "No. Not at all," he finally said.

"See. You're fine," Kyle agreed, but I knew different.

Back at Kyle's, we both prepared to take our tests. It was more stressful than the SATs. He cracked open a beer and said, "I'll go first." I did deep breathing while he went into the bathroom and peed on the magic wand. A second later, he emerged.

"Well, mine is negative!" he announced cheerily. "Your turn."

As I got up to go to the loo, the buzzer rang. It was Kyle's delightfully eccentric mother, Rose, unexpectedly dropping by for a glass of wine. She was tiny, not more than 5 feet tall; a sixty-something retired secretary with long, white hair she wore in a bun. Kyle had inherited her smile, her elfin eyes, her sense of humor and her fierceness. Rose was like a younger Greenwich Village version of Granny from the *Beverly Hillbillies.*

"What are you kids up to?" she asked, taking a seat as Kyle poured her a glass of wine and put out a cheese plate.

"Well, Alice here was about to take a pregnancy test."

"Oh boy."

"Oh boy is right," I said.

"Maybe you shouldn't be drinking," she said, motioning to the six-pack.

"I'm not." Truth was, since the "incident" I hadn't wanted a drink or smoke.

"Good."

Kyle turned on a TV Music channel to try to lighten the mood. It didn't help, as "Midnight Train to Georgia," one of the saddest songs ever written, came on. It made a potentially depressing situation miraculously even more depressing.

"I suppose I should get on with it," I said, carrying my wand of doom into the bathroom. Rose and Kyle crossed their fingers and furrowed their brows in exactly the same manner.

The fact that I now had an audience and a soundtrack made me pee shy. Kyle's mom was a cool lady but I worried what she would think of me. I never stupidly relied on the "pull-out" method. I always used condoms and I wanted her to know that, to know I was responsible in at least one aspect of my messy life. I know too many women who wound up playing "guess the daddy" when they missed their periods. It was a game I never wanted to play.

It took me a minute to muster up the courage to pee but once I did, the result was hardly a surprise—one bright pink strip, irreversible and terrifying. I sat down on the toilet and cried until Kyle knocked on the door.

"You OK?" he asked.

"Uh-uh." My whole body shook as I opened the door.

"It's gonna be all right," he said, as I fell into his arms and sobbed.

"Please, please, please turn this fucking music off," I said.

"Oh Jesus. I'm sorry," he said.

"Alice, honey, it's gonna be OK," Rose added while Kyle rushed to the TV and tried to remedy the situation by putting on a wacky Partridge Family CD. But not even David Cassidy could stop my tears.

We conferred about what I should do next. Opening the phone book, I wrote down the number of a nearby clinic since getting a "real" pregnancy test was necessary no matter what decision I eventually made.

Two days later, the clinic confirmed what I'd know since the condom broke—I was pregnant.

I scheduled an abortion, to be performed the following week, on July 3rd. The cost was four-hundred dollars, five-hundred if you wanted to be anaesthetized. I splurged on the anesthesia. Despite all the pain I'd endured at the dungeon, I didn't want to feel one second of this kind of pain. I wanted to disappear along with the child I would never have.

I'd never wanted to be a mother, wife or even a girlfriend. I'd only ever wanted to be one thing—an artist. And this was a role I equated with absolute freedom; freedom that I wasn't about to give up for a child. Despite this, the decision hurt like nothing else. Pro-lifers call women who have abortions "murderers." I didn't feel like a murderer, but I did feel like I was making a huge sacrifice.

I told myself that maybe when I got older, when I "made it" and had five million dollars in the bank, I'd adopt a child and give him or her a loving home. I told myself a lot of things to make myself feel better. I tried to stay busy. I went to museums. I went for long walks and went to the zoo even though zoos always seemed like "animal jail" to me. I watched the exquisite captive creatures, caring for their young instinctively even in their ridiculous habitats. The tiny Black Lion Tamarin monkeys had faces like old men, even the babies. Under their cage it said there were only six hundred or so left in existence. I wondered why there couldn't be just six-hundred humans. Things would be so much easier and none of the animals would be in jail.

I didn't tell my parents I was pregnant but I did tell my sister, who sent me two hundred dollars cash, folded in a short note. She was busy planning her wedding at the time, preparing to have a normal family while I was solidifying my aloneness. She understood and supported my decision. I also told Dylan, Tommy and eventually Stu.

Stu's reaction stunned me. "How do I know you're telling the truth?" he asked.

"Do you want me to pee on a fucking stick in front of you?"

"No. It's just I had one girlfriend who faked a pregnancy so I would stay with her once."

"Well, I'm not that girlfriend and I don't expect you to stay. I don't expect a fucking thing from you. Do what you like."

Stu didn't need to hear this. He would always do what he liked no matter what. He would always abandon me when I was at my weakest because he wasn't strong enough to support me and he would abandon me when I was strong because he envied my strength.

Hence I didn't invite Stu along for my "imaginary" abortion. He had to work that day anyway since his weed wasn't gonna buy itself. Instead, I brought Dylan who insisted on going with me. The clinic was completely ghetto, everything in it pink, plastic, uncomfortable and lined with filth, like a post-apocalyptic Barbie Dream House. I was called into a private waiting room where I sat with at least six other women who were also scheduled to have abortions. We all must've sat there for over five hours discussing our soon-to-be-terminated pregnancies before we were given assless paper gowns along with paper slippers and led into the operating room. It was one enormous room containing several gurneys, each partitioned off by a curtain. I lay down on my appointed gurney and awaited my anesthesia. It was freezing cold and I asked for a blanket. They brought me a paper one and then they gently put me to sleep.

When I woke up I was no longer pregnant. I looked down and noticed my arm was bleeding.

"Why is my arm bleeding?" I asked the nurse.

"The syringe—You pulled away when I tried to remove the syringe."

"Syringe?"

"Valium."

"Thank God for that."

I was confused and shivering under the paper blanket. I wanted my real clothes. I wanted my shoes. I wanted a hug. I wanted hope. I wanted never to be anaesthetized again, never to sleep again. I wanted to feel everything. I don't believe life begins at conception but I do believe that at conception, the universe offers you a chance to bring life into the world. I had rejected that offer for the sake of my own life. I had no regrets though I felt empty, starved and weak and I desperately wanted to see Dylan. The transition from conscious to unconscious and back again in under an hour is overwhelming; the transition from pregnant to not pregnant in under twenty minutes, more so. The surgery had been at once physically simple and emotionally complicated.

The nurse brought me an oatmeal cookie. I think it was Amway, but it was stale. I ate it anyway as my arm continued to bleed dark, burgundy blood. Eventually they gave me my clothes, told me I could dress and go outside. The waiting room was filled with men, none of them smoking celebratory cigars. They looked about as cheerful as the old men at Rudy's. Dylan was waiting for me amongst the boyfriends, somehow fitting since she'd once fucked me with a fake penis.

"Jesus Christ! That took forever!" She said. "I pictured you lying on a gurney telling the candy asses to move it."

"Wasn't quite that dramatic, but they did play some serious drag-ass. Then when they finally did it, took about ten minutes."

"Well, let's get you out of this shit-hole. You'd think, charging what they do, they could hire someone to clean."

Dylan offered to get me a cab, but I wanted to walk home, to feel the sunshine on my face. We picked up my prescriptions, some pills to make me bleed less and some other pills I can't remember. The after-care instructions, suggested no alcohol for at least twenty-four hours. This, I ignored completely, picking up a few tall boys to go with the pills. They'd help wash down the pills along with the terrible loneliness that would soon engulf me.

For twenty-four hours I waited for Stu to call or arrive at my door or show that he cared in some small way. Tommy and Kyle called and Jake brought me dinner from the restaurant where he worked, but it was Stu's voice I wanted to hear and didn't.

It was 4th of July. I was invited to barbeques, to shows and to Coney Island, but I just wanted to stay home with my notebook and crippling depression. At twilight, I tried to go up to my roof. My landlord had locked it. Undeterred, I climbed out my bedroom window and dangerously scaled the world's most rickety fire escape. The roof was abandoned, my own little place of contemplation. Fireflies buzzed around and car alarms screamed below. Other than that, the city was still. People were either gathered at the East River preparing to watch fireworks or at parties.

I contemplated jumping. I'd fallen so deep down the rabbit hole, I couldn't find my way out and wasn't sure what to do next. I was a prostitute who'd just had an abortion and had been abandoned by my lover when I needed him most. Others told me I was a brilliant artist, but I was living hand to mouth and getting no responses from the magazines I'd queried. Things were certainly not going well, but I had two things going for me, two things that would continually save me, that would ensure I never jumped to an untimely death. The first was freedom. I had nothing left to lose and therefore everything to gain. The second was curiosity. Curiosity would always be the thing that got me into trouble and it would always be the thing that saved me. The same curiosity that brought me into the sex industry would get me out. I would never give up, never jump, never throw my life away, simply because I wondered—*What's next?*

## Chapter 26

## *Goodbye*

My twenty-fifth birthday fell on the coldest, rainiest day in July. My "party" was at Motor City, a rock 'n' roll bar on Ludlow Street not vile enough to be a dive bar, but pretty close. Plenty of friends showed up, bearing unusual presents (porn mags, poppers, etc.) Kyle made me a chocolate cake covered with rainbow sprinkles since one of my mottos is "sprinkles should be on everything." Along with the cake, Kyle provided plastic forks and knives with penis-shaped handles that came in a bag labeled "Penis Cutlery." We daintily ate the cake with our penises whilst undaintily downing numerous pints. (People who say beer and cake don't go together aren't real beer drinkers. Beer goes with everything.) Tommy and Kyle gave me a pricey vibrator dildo with a clitoral stimulator attachment shaped like a polar bear. When you pressed one button, the little bear's tongue darted up and down. When you pressed another button, the dildo, which had a tiki doll face, yet was shaped like a penis, swiveled around and changed directions. They were thoughtful enough to also get me lube and batteries. (Since one of the certainties in life, right after death and taxes, is that toys never come with batteries.) Kyle made the card. On the frois isnt, he'd written "He's really sorry he's too busy running the business to make it here tonight" and on the inside, he wrote, "But your boyfriend wanted us to tell you he misses and loves you very much." Next to this, there was a picture of an elderly toothless man holding a picture of Elvis and standing in front of the "Elvis Museum." This was an extension of our favorite game, "There's your boyfriend" which is normally played by twelve-year-old girls. Playing is simple. You just find the least suited to be a boyfriend person readily apparent to the naked eye and you say, "Oh my God! There's your boyfriend!" It can also be played as "There's your mom!" or even, on long road trips, as "There's your house!"

It's important to get creative with it by elaborating on said "boyfriend." If you see a crazy looking old fart wearing a fanny pack, you can say, "I like your boyfriend's fanny pack! Is that where he keeps his lube?"

The tiki doll-faced vibrator was attracting everyone's attention, so much so, that the bouncer came over to inspect it with his flashlight.

"That is some piece of equipment," he said.

I agreed. "I don't know of a single human penis that can do all this. And it's kind of adorable too."

Stu eventually showed up. I'd seen him twice since the abortion. We didn't talk much about what happened and we didn't fight. Though I was still depressed and angry, I didn't have the energy for drama.

He arrived empty-handed and nodding out, his head flopping back and forth while everyone else was having a good time. I wasn't sure if he was on drugs or just drunk, tired and bored.

Finally, he nudged me. "C'mon let's go," he said. I looked at my crazy friends dancing around, doing shots and laughing. I wanted to be with them but I also wanted intimacy. I wanted to be held and fucked. And that's all it took for me to say goodnight and leave the bar.

At home Stu and I got undressed and got in to bed. He never said, "Happy Birthday" and he never gave me a card or any little thing to show he cared. Anything would have been acceptable—a Little Debbie snack cake with a candle in it or even a can of Budweiser with a bow on it or even a can of Budweiser with no bow.

Suddenly I felt pissed off. What I wanted—to be held and fucked was an extension of the desire to feel adored. And I didn't feel that. In fact, I felt like shit.

"Listen, I'm not trying to be a prima donna but you didn't get me shit all for my birthday," I said abruptly.

"I feel bad. I'll make it up to you."

"You could have given me a hug. I would have taken a hug. Anything."

"Listen, Alice, can we just go to bed? I'm tired."

"You dragged me away from my friends so we could sleep?"

"Yeah. I'm exhausted and honestly, *you* invited me. It was all your idea. Most of the time, it's your idea."

"WHAT is *all my idea?*"

"When we hook up. I've been ready to break up with you for months, but you just come on so strong and I can't resist you."

"All right. I'm gonna ask you something and I need an honest answer."

"What?"

"Do you love me?"

He was silent.

"Do you fucking love me?" I asked again.

"I'm tired of this conversation."

"I need to know if you love me."

"Not enough. No. I don't love you enough."

"OK. Then you have to leave."

Wordlessly, he put on his clothes and walked to the door.

"Goodbye," I said as he walked out.

"Goodbye," he said and didn't look back.

I knew then that we would never be together again. My chest ached until the aching reached my eyes and the tears started to flow. I still longed for his touch, and I would for a long time. I didn't like to think of him walking home in the cold July rain, but I knew one thing—whereas I was sobbing, I was certain he hadn't shed a tear.

Being with Stu, whose love and attention was so inconsistent, required more strength than I could continue to give. And thanks to my incredible friends, I now had a swiveling, vibrating dildo that only required batteries, which were easily gotten at the bodega. That was about all I could handle. I was through with unhealthy love, drama and codependency.

Codependency, I realized, is what happens when two people constantly say, "fuck you" instead of "goodbye." "Fuck you" is easier because two people can exchange fuck yous for a lifetime but you can only really say goodbye once. Goodbye, when it's real, is final.

## Chapter 27

## *Just a Notch (on an Extremely Heavy Belt)*

I was done with codependency but I certainly wasn't done with beer. After Stu left, I cried some more, put some refrigerated moisturizer under my eyes to reduce the swelling, threw on my clothes and went back to the bar. Things were wilder than before. Kyle had taken E and was making out with a random brunette in the corner. Tommy, meanwhile, was playing Pac-Man on the bar's sit down video arcade console with a look of fascinated delight painted across his face. I grabbed a pint and sat across from him.

I told him what had just gone down with Stu.

"Don't worry, baby. Everything will be all right. You'll be in pain for like six months, but after that, you'll be all right."

"Why six months?"

"Because that's how long it generally takes to get over someone. In six months, I guarantee you pick up an old journal and can't even remember who this 'Stu' was you kept writing about."

"That's the good thing about old journals. When you look at them, you can see that though your life is pathetic now, it was once *more* pathetic."

"And you can read about all the foolish mistakes you

made in the past and then go out and repeat them again and again."

"Not me. I am staying away from dudes forever."

"Alice, you are way too young to have a monogamous relationship with your dildo."

"I'm not young! I'm twenty-five!"

"You're a baby! I'm thirty-three, balding and now carrying ten extra pounds, which I tell the 'ladies' I've gained for a 'role.' They don't realize the 'role' is that of a barely employed writer with a drinking problem."

"Yeah, but women age in dog years, which is actually fine with me. I'm tired of being Lolita. I can't wait till I'm an old lady."

"Alice, honey, you already are. You're the foxiest old lady on the block."

"Thanks."

"Look at me."

I looked at Tommy.

"There are three things in my life," he said as he stretched his arms across the Pac-Man console and held onto my hands. "There's writing. There's the sauce and there's you, but mostly, there's just you."

"I love you, Tommy. And that's not a drunk 'I love you, Man', but a real one."

"I love you too, which is why I'll never try to hold onto you. You've gotta go out there and live like crazy and fill your journals with stupid experience after stupid experience until you've got something that resembles a book. It's our job as writers to be fools."

"Well, I'm certainly an expert at it. I was foolish enough to fall for Stu's bullshit. I wish he'd just gone ahead and fucked me, but there were times when he was romantic, when he'd chill a tall boy for me in an ice bucket, cook dinner for me and kiss me sweetly and say the things I wanted to hear. I knew it was a weird little act, but I suspended my disbelief and went with it like he was *E.T.* or the Last fucking Unicorn because I desperately needed some magic. And now I'm just a notch on his belt, his ridiculously heavy belt."

"Yeah, it's like a janitorial utility belt."

"And the keys are like the souls and hearts of all the women in the East Village he's broken."

"Soon enough that belt will weigh him down. You might have been a fool for him but at least you don't have to carry around that kind of weight."

"Well, tonight I feel lighter than ever, like I just lost one-hundred-and-fifty pounds of scrawny musician. You know what that motherfucker said to me?"

"Oh God. Not sure I wanna hear."

"He said it was all my idea—us fucking."

"Yeah. Every time he got a stiffie, it was your idea. You don't need that douche."

The bar was increasingly raucous. Random bargoers were helping themselves to cake. Tommy and I watched in horror as a large biker reached his visibly filthy hands directly into the cake and started tearing off pieces.

"Oh my God! That biker dude just raped your cake!" Tommy exclaimed.

"My cake has been assaulted."

"Did he not notice the penis cutlery?"

We were seized by uncontrollable laughter especially when we saw Kyle noticing the cake's demise. There was nothing we could do, given the cake rapist was three hundred pounds of pure muscle.

Eventually, a slow song came on—the Beatles version of "You Really Got a Hold on Me"—and everyone got up to dance. It was like a prom for misfits. Tommy and I rose from the Pac-Man console and swayed to the music, pressing close together. I felt light on my feet, happy and certain I'd made the right choice. The freedom to be foolish meant everything.

## Chapter 28

## *All My Idea*

*I* didn't fancy myself a poet. In fact, what I'd been writing mostly was pornography, which I dutifully continued to send out to porn mags, hoping for a paycheck—one that didn't require taking my clothes off but *writing* about taking my clothes off. Still, when Stu dumped me, the floodgates of poetry opened, possibly because it's difficult to write pornography when you're angry and heartbroken. Turns out, Stu hurt me so deeply I was able to write a short book of poems about the pain and anger. I called the book *Bad for my Liver. Good for My Art* since I'd been on something of a bender since the breakup (as if I hadn't already.) Luckily, it was a prolific bender.

On hung over mornings when I wasn't needed at a session, I lay in bed and, in a cheery green notebook with the phrase "Supergirlistic" printed all over it in rainbow bubble letters, I wrote poetry, sobbing dramatically as I did. Though what Stu and I had was so open as to almost be a "fake relationship" the way it ended and the way he behaved before, during and after the abortion, left me crushed. And there are only two ways I know how to deal with being crushed—writing and drinking. I made copies of *Bad for my*

*Liver. Good for My Art* at Kinkos, bound them with a stapler and sold them at the open mikes. People responded to the poems and I made about fifty bucks in the process. Some of the poems were completely sophomoric—*If Mercury is out of Retrograde, Why do I Still Feel like Uranus?* Some were short—*It IS You, Not me*—"It IS you, not me. You are really, truly fucked up." And, some, when I look back, remind me of how much it hurts to lose a lover—*All My Idea*.

### *All My Idea*
*Clearly, it was all my idea*
*When you flipped me over*
*And spanked my ass*
*And pulled my hair*
*And filled 100 condoms*
*With enough seminal fluid*
*To irrigate a small village*

*Obviously, I wanted it more than you*
*Each time you called me up*
*And requested a long, hot kiss*
*Or an escape between my thighs*

*When you told me I was*
*The sexiest creature you'd ever*
*Laid eyes or hands on*
*How you wished*
*I was there in your bed*
*How you were going to dream*

*About kissing my neck*
*And cuddling*
*Next to my naked body*

*This morning, woke up*
*Feeling sick to my stomach*
*Feeling lied to*
*Feeling cheated*
*Like I gave you*
*The best I had to offer*
*Which was pretending*
*I'd never been hurt*
*I risked my pride*
*Letting you see*
*That I wanted to be loved*
*And in return*
*I got a game*
*I couldn't play*

*You told me*
*You would kill*
*For an afternoon with me*
*To get your hands on my soft skin*
*Around my little waist*

*But clearly*
*I inconvenienced you*
*With my ankles around your neck*
*Giving you that*

*Long, hot kiss*
*You requested so many times*

*I feel like a fool*
*Which is not as bad*
*As the regret you'll feel*
*When you miss those afternoons*
*Those long, hot kisses*
*The soft skin*
*My broken box spring*
*And my broken heart*
*Until then*
*Tell yourself*
*It was all my idea.*

## Chapter 29

## *The Mirror*

Getting over Stu took less than six months. Writing helped. And so did Tommy and Kyle. They were amazed that I could write poetry that was both "jackable" and heartbreaking. And they both told me to keep writing and just keep being. As I had encouraged Kyle to stay alive during his stint at the nuthouse, so he encouraged me. I'd tried to break him out of the nuthouse and he prevented me from going in.

"Just *be*, Alice. And the world will fall breathless at your feet," he said.

"I'm doing too much being and not enough thinking," I said.

I was always just being, always just staying in the same place in my little cramped quarters on the Lower East Side, where the ceiling was caving in and the rats in the hallway were fucking more than me and the sound from the Williamsburg Bridge and traffic kept me up all night. I just stayed there waiting for someone to come along and save, fuck, feed or kiss me or even take me away against my will. I didn't really want to leave the Lower East Side; I just wanted life to be less insane there. What I didn't realize yet is that I was the only one who could make it less insane.

"No one here is led from a path of righteous self control because no one comes here to exercise self control," Kyle once said to me.

We'd all been led to the Lower East Side because we were bohemians and just like every generation of bohemians that had come before us, we were fucking nuts.

I was still dependent on the sex industry since regular employers weren't buying my phony résumé and if they were, it wasn't even good enough. My feelings of empathy toward my clients were starting to turn into feelings of rage. Instead of nightmares where Sheldon was trying to rape me, I had dreams where I was punching him in the face repeatedly. What I hated most was how so many of them deluded themselves into thinking I liked the sessions. Yes, sometimes I got wet but that is how my body is designed to work during sexual contact. I later learned that it's not entirely uncommon for a woman to have an orgasm during rape or abuse. Doesn't mean she liked it, just means her body reacted physically.

There were plenty of final straws, insults to my time and intelligence. One was a call from Bradley.

"Have you been tested lately?" he asked.

In fact, I had been tested for *everything* at Gouverneur, the sliding scale clinic in Chinatown. I told him this and also reminded him that we'd only practiced safe sex.

"Well, it's just that I noticed something..."

"On your penis?"

"Yeah. It's like really red, like a rash."

"Did *you* get tested?"

"No. Not yet. I just wondered do you think you might have syphilis?"

Syphilis was making a "comeback" in the mid-nineties along with lots of other old-timey things like absinthe. Everyone was on high alert for symptoms and they automatically tested you for it at the clinic.

"Wait. Why do you think you have syphilis?"

"One of the symptoms is a rash."

"You don't think maybe you gave yourself a rash jacking off with moisturizer?"

"Well, it could be that."

"Maybe you ought to go to a doctor. Don't you have other lovers?"

"Yeah, but they're really normal."

"So you don't think a normal girl could give you syphilis?"

"Don't take it the wrong way. It's just that I know you fool around."

"Don't worry, Bradley. I know I'm not normal and I also know I don't have syphilis. You should probably go to a doctor and you should probably buy some water-based lube."

We said goodbye cordially but the entire exchange infuriated me. He had it in his head that only weird, artistic girls could give him syphilis.

"There's nothing funny about syphilis, but the whole thing is kind of hilarious," Dylan said a few nights later when she stopped by for a beer. "What a drama queen."

"Well then, he called back two days later and said 'not to worry' it was just a rash. Of course it was just a fucking rash. He jacks off with that crap from the 99-Cent Store!"

"What a douche."

Dylan had stopped seeing Bradley, not just because she thought he was a douche; but because she met someone while she was dancing at the club. (Men—These stories are one in a million. You should never try to work a stripper.) Jeffrey was a kindhearted lawyer with a foot-fetish and enough money to take care of Dylan while she made art full-time. He didn't demand monogamy of her and she didn't practice it though she truly loved him. They lived together in a huge apartment in Park Slope, which Dylan had tricked out in the most over-the-top Goth manner imaginable. A few years later, Kyle and I would even be bridesmaids at their wedding in Vegas.

Because Jeffrey took good care of Dylan, she took good care of her friends. On the night she stopped by, she brought me a late birthday present—a vintage light-up makeup mirror she'd gotten at a flea market. I'd always wanted one.

"Now I can really look at myself!" I said, gasping with joy as I placed it atop the old vanity I'd found on the street and dragged up to my apartment. And later that night, after Dylan left, I sat at my vanity, turned on the mirror and *really* looked at myself. Despite all the hours spent dressing and undressing and getting made-up for others, I barely looked at myself. I decided a while ago that I was neither a true narcissist or my own worst critic but basically someone who just deals with myself. It's at least better than hating myself.

In the mirror, I studied my enlarged pores, my freckles and my tiredness. On the surface, I was still a Lolita but my eyes told a different story. They looked like they wanted to close and sleep for hours while the bags under them looked like they wanted to stay up all night telling stories.

My reflection's message was simple. My Lolita days were numbered, but I'd be better off for it because my Artist days would last forever.

Looking around the apartment, I found proof of this everywhere, in my paintings and in the journals stacked up on my nightstand. The past year and a half hadn't been entirely wasted. Despite the mayhem and turmoil I'd experienced, and despite partying as only an untaxed, cash-carrying twentysomething can, I'd been prolific. The money I'd earned from the wealthy, the bankers and the bishop, had afforded me the time to paint and had paid for my art supplies. And just as artists hundreds of years ago had done with money from the banks and the churches, I'd painted classical themes and portraits. I'd just begun painting Dylan as Venus rising from the East River, flanked by a rat on one side and a pigeon on the other. The piece was ostensibly titled "Venus of the East River" and I'd carefully stretched it on black velvet instead of canvas. The painting of Jake as Pan, the God of Nature, was finally complete. He danced on goat legs, playing his pipes and staring at me with twinkling eyes. Picasso once said, "Painting is just another way of keeping a diary," so it was no wonder I'd painted Pan and Venus, renowned for their sexual prowess. They were Gods before chastity was equated with moral quality, Gods from a time before Adam and Eve had to put on their clothes and get the hell out of Eden, before we were taught to hate our bodies and hide our transgressions in dungeons. These were the Gods I still worshipped.

## Chapter 30

## *The Next Trap*

Not long after Dylan's visit and my meditation upon the magic mirror, I found myself back at the nameless dungeon in need of cash. It was the end of August and rent was due. Rent was a force almost as powerful as gravity. Once a month, it brought me to my knees, sometimes literally. Annie told me Lord H was in the Dominican Republic enslaving girls with even less to lose than us. Bradley still called but after his unfounded syphilis accusation, I wasn't too jazzed to see him. So the kooky nameless dungeon it was. I took the subway there, just for the air conditioning, since it was an unbearably hot afternoon and I was unbearably hung over.

In one trembling hand, I held a can of Coke, in the other a copy of *The Art of War*. Why was I reading this? For what war was I preparing? It just seemed like one of those books everyone should read.

My glazed eyes stared at the page. "An exhausted animal will still fight, as a matter of natural law." That's how I felt—like an exhausted animal seeing how long I could keep going in the battle to exist. But, even if I were to "win" would I still be engulfed by memories of this battle? Would memory cripple me from feeling at ease in the future? That day, I felt like I could just lie down on the subway and give up trying to live a life. Let them take me away, put me in an institution and put a straightjacket on me so I couldn't touch anyone including myself, just so long as I could get some rest.

I was momentarily cheered up when a man got on at 14th Street and announced to everyone on the train that his name was "Swiss Cheese" and that he was selling candy to try to raise money to go on his senior class trip to Rome, Italy. He looked like he was about foty-five.

An elderly Asian man wearing a shirt that said, "It's not me, it's you" gave him a dollar.

Swiss Cheese disembarked at 34th Street, as did I. Within minutes of entering the dungeon's seedy interior, I had a client. He was decent, a newbie who was into role play.

One of the first things he asked me was, "Are you in love?"

"No," I answered.

"Good. Have you ever been in love?"

"Yes."

"Are you a cynic?"

"You only have to get your heart broken once to be a cynic."

"Good answer. Are you Irish?"

"My grandparents were."

"Perfect. We're gonna go back about two-hundred years then and you are going to be my little Irish servant girl."

I imagined my Irish ancestors rolling in their graves. He was of course, a dashing English Lord though in reality he was a plump, middle-aged man from New Jersey. He'd brought along a medieval-looking corset he'd likely acquired at a Ren Faire, which he told me to wear over lingerie.

I changed in the waiting room then returned to the small room where my Lord was waiting, flogger in hand. He tied me up, flogged and spanked me, all while accusing me of being a Witch. I claimed to be a good Christian servant girl and begged his mercy. Funny thing is, though my parents were both atheists, I was certain many of my ancestors were actually Witches. Through Crowley, I'd become interested in Wicca and through books about Wicca I was slowly learning enough about the Craft that I hoped to someday follow in their footsteps. My maternal grandmother, Bernadette, in particular, had always seemed like a Witch. She had naturally jet-black hair, a pronounced wart above her left eyebrow and a talent for reading tarot cards that attracted even the most "Christian" ladies to her tiny house. She cut her bangs severely short so everyone could see her wart. "That way everyone knows I'm a Witch," she'd say, only half-joking. When she swooshed into a room, you could feel her energy. I wish I'd gotten to know her better, to learn all of her secrets, but she died when I was very young. One thing I instinctively did know about her was that she was nobody's servant. I always wanted to be like her and even bought a pack of Tarot Cards when I was twelve, but I didn't have the patience to read them. Even Witchcraft, I realized later, required discipline. But in the dungeon's land of make-believe, it was easy.

Finally, I broke down in front of the mighty English Lord. "All right! I am a Witch!" I blurted out.

He'd known all along, he said and then proceeded to beat my ass until the CD ended and I had to break the fourth wall to our audience of no one and explain that our time was up.

Back in the waiting room, everyone was glued to the TV, watching a PBS documentary about orchids. Because no one in the waiting room ever spoke to me and because I forgot my book, I watched along with them—the two junkies who were barely staying awake and the speed freak who was completely transfixed. I didn't think I gave a shit about orchids, but after a minute, I was transfixed too. Turns out orchids are not all pretty smelling like roses are, but some smell downright disgusting. One smelled like rotting flesh (which attracted flies), another smelled like raspberries and another like coconuts. But the most fascinating orchids featured had pools of sticky nectar at their center. The narrator explained that bees and butterflies dive into them to suck the nectar out and they get stuck—they drown to death in the sweet nectar.

Just as I was thinking *not a bad way to go*, they showed footage of a bee stuck in the nectar struggling to free itself. It reminded me of a mouse trying to free itself from a glue trap. (This was something I'd been unfortunate enough to witness in the hallway of my building. If the mouse is not injured, you can free it from glue trap peril using vegetable oil. Unfortunately, this guy was partially dismembered but still fighting and whimpering. I threw him/her to a merciful death out the window, said a prayer for its little rodent soul then succinctly removed all the glue traps from the hallway.) But back to the bee, it was struggling as the mouse had done and I found myself crying over its anguish. Embarrassed, I tried to brush away my tears before anyone noticed (not that anyone there noticed anything) but tears were soon gushing out of my eyes. Not sure why, when I watch the news about a terrible plane crash where hundreds of people die, I don't always cry but show me a National Geographic documentary where one tiger cub gets bitten by a snake and dies and I cry for hours. I didn't even cry when Elvis died and here I was crying over a bee.

Amazingly enough, the bee freed itself from the sticky nectar. My heart soared over its emancipation and I watched its next moves closely. What would it do now that it had cheated death? The first thing it did was give itself a bath. And the second thing it did was dive into yet another flower and get stuck once again.

Looking around the waiting room, I wondered if anyone else noticed the parallel between the bee and us. They all had their sticky nectar and so did I. Whether it was speed, heroin, beer, writing or just not having to punch a clock, each of us there was all too willing to dive into the next trap.

## Chapter 31

## *Never*

When Lord H returned from the Dominican Republic, Annie and Luna went to Paris for a two-week vacation. Without Annie in New York City, H grew antsy and asked to see me alone. I knew it would be unbearably painful, almost an act of lunacy to see him solo, but he made an offer I couldn't refuse—one thousand dollars for the hour plus the rental fee for Avalon. This amount of money meant one thing to me—freedom. It was more than two months rent, two months when I'd be able to look for a job, any shit job, so that I wouldn't suffocate in the next pool of seemingly sweet nectar.

There are some things we completely block out of memory so as not to go insane and most of the hour I spent alone with H falls into that blackout zone. I turned off my senses and tried hard not to smell, feel or see him.

He started the session by unpacking his toy bag and announcing, "We're going to have some fun today!" while pulling out an assortment of dildos, crops, canes and of course, the hairbrush.

*Correction, Lord H, I thought, YOU are going to have some fun today. I'm going to survive today and then I'm going to walk as fast as fuck home, give myself a bath and never be the receptacle for your fucked-upedness again. So help me Goddess. Amen.*

He was already undressed and I was already dressed in a navy blue schoolgirl uniform when he ordered me onto my hands and knees on top of the leather bed. Then, without warning, he forced my panties aside, lubed up a dildo and forced it inside of my pussy. He jabbed it in and out of me with absolutely no concern for my pleasure then pulled it out and thrust it into my mouth.

"Don't drop it," he warned as he began to assault my ass with his hand. I struggled to keep the dildo locked between my lips, feeling like an idiot as I did. (I already felt like an idiot for having agreed to the solo session, but this made me feel even stupider.) I survived the exercise and he told me to stand in front of him. When I did, he slipped a blindfold over my eyes, pulled my panties off and proceeded to maniacally finger-fuck my unlubricated pussy before suggesting I get on my knees and show him pleasure. As I attempted to fellate his flaccid cock, he fastened a collar and leash to my neck. Tugging on the leash, he told me to follow him on my hands and knees.

When he stopped, he told me to lie down. I lay on my back and he fastened cuffs to my ankles. I was disoriented from both the blindfold and the fear and had no idea what was about to happen.

Then, slowly, I felt myself being hoisted into the air by my ankles until I was upside down, with my waist-long hair just barely sweeping the floor.

"No, no, no, no," I protested.

"Don't panic," he said, but the blood was rushing to my head and I was sure this would lead to an aneurysm.

I cried "no" again and that's when I felt the cane come down hard, first on my ass and then on my legs. My legs. A cane. It would leave marks the way he was wielding it. Red stripes, blue marks and in between, my pasty white flesh—my very own freak flag. I loved showing off the legs I'd earned from my brutal walk-up. They were the strongest part of my body and almost always, the first thing men noticed about me. I wasn't going to let him fuck them up for any amount of money. Vanity, apparently, is where I draw the line.

"Stop that now," I said in a voice you might use with a disobedient child.

"Don't be a baby," he said.

"Stop that now or I will *never* see you again," I added. Little did he know, he never *would* see me again.

The threat worked. He stopped. It was the first battle I'd won with H. He lowered me and undid the ankle cuffs.

As I lay on the cold floor, still blindfolded, H lifted up my skirt and began to eat my pussy. His rough beard scratched the insides of my thighs as his index finger worked its way inside my asshole. He eventually pulled his finger out and brought it to my lips.

"Taste yourself," he said and I did. I tasted okay, much better than I expected.

He then removed the blindfold and led me to a leather couch where he sat down. Bending me over his knee, he began the cruel and unusual punishment I was more familiar with. He spanked me until tears welled up in my eyes and eventually brought the hairbrush down on me. As always, the hairbrush ritual culminated in his orgasm. It was an orgasm born from his self-hatred, the product of terrible abuse. And though I sometimes felt rage toward him, I still felt sorry for him, even at the end. Since Annie told me about his mother beating him and his sister, I couldn't look at him without thinking of the wonderful child he must've been and the wonderful man he could have turned out to be if he'd been taught with love instead of fear. But I couldn't help him; I could only help myself and that's why I had to get the hell away from him as quickly as possible.

I dressed, left Avalon and raced to a bank where I deposited the one thousand dollars like it was stolen money. From there, I race-walked back to the Lower East Side, praying I'd never have to step foot above 14th Street again.

# Chapter 32

## *Eden*

"It's the Garden of Eden and anything goes."
—Jack Kerouac, *Desolation Angels*

I lay in the bathtub and looked at my legs through the water. The cane had left marks, but they wouldn't last. They were stripes, like an old-fashioned prison uniform, and I figured once they vanished, it'd be like the jailer unlocking the key and granting me definitive freedom.

I had promised myself that once I quit, the first thing I'd do would be to take a bath. That part was easy—soaking in the tub and feeling triumphant, but there were plenty of other steps, both practical and symbolic, that I had to take to ensure I wouldn't be lured back.

The most practical of them was that I had to change my phone number. This irked me primarily because I had a 212 area code and changing my number meant getting a new 646 area code. I knew Jake wouldn't be happy about adopting an uncool area code, but uncoolness was a small price to pay for creepy men not calling night and day, requesting sex for money or asking if I had syphilis.

Symbolically, I had to get rid of the things that represented "June"—the schoolgirl getup, brush and ring H had given me, my mary janes and bobby socks and all the other knickknacks I'd picked up.

The only things I would keep were the paintings I'd done along the way and the journals I'd kept. The journals were sporadically written. Months had been skipped and details left out, but they were proof. The dream people who promised to take my pain away had told me, "Remember your life." I answered that I had no memories and they asked, "Then how do you know you lived?" These journals were the only answer I could give them. I had not only lived, I had lived through this.

I drained the tub and stood up. Turning on the shower, I said a cleansing prayer that a Puerto Rican Witch once taught me—*"In the Name of the Holy Mystery, I wash today's shit off of me!"*

I imagined every terrible thing I'd felt that day and over the past two years going down the drain along with the soapy water. Once I was sufficiently clean, I stepped out, dried off and threw on an old pair of jeans and my tattered Yoda t-shirt.

Tearing a piece of paper from one of my journals, I sat down at my kitchen table with a Flair pen. I was going to write a letter of resignation, something to tack on my wall as a reminder that "June" no longer existed. I was unsure what to write or who to write it to, but soon found myself jotting something down in bold letters, one sentence that formed from the wellsprings of my subconscious, one promise that

I would abide to—*Dear Venus, I promise to never sell my body again if you grant me stability as an artist.*

Intuitively, I knew Venus was the perfect deity to whom I should address the letter since she represents beauty, love and desire. She's also benevolent toward artists who seek her help. When Pygmalion left Venus offerings, she responded by turning the sculpture he loved into a real woman. I wasn't asking nearly as much, yet I'd just made a pact with a Goddess and you don't break a pact, especially one with a Goddess.

Maybe I was crazy for writing letters to a Goddess, but it seemed no crazier than when Margaret talked to God about getting her period. In fact, lots of people try to talk to God. They just normally go to church to do it.

I hung my resignation letter over my desk and for the first time in two years, I had complete faith that somehow, the universe would provide for me. I would be okay.

I picked up the phone to call AT&T when the buzzer rang. "Who is it?"

"It's Tommy. I brought you blinner."

Blinner was the one meal a day we generally made time for—breakfast, lunch and dinner combined. I buzzed him in and a few minutes later he arrived at my door carrying a gigantic watermelon and a bag of groceries. He heaved the melon onto my kitchen table.

"Jesus H. Christ! I barely got that thing up your stairs," he said, sighing dramatically as he lit up a Marlboro Red. "How *do* you climb Mount Alice every day? Summer's almost over so I thought we should eat some summer foods. We can eat the watermelon with sporks. It's more fun that way."

He proceeded to pull out a random assortment of groceries—grapes, cheese, crackers, dark chocolate, a twelve-pack of Budweiser and plastic-wrapped sporks, all while talking at a rapid pace.

"I was gonna try to get a bottle of rum to pour into the watermelon, but I know you don't really do the hard stuff," he explained. "Also, what if you poke holes in the watermelon, pour the rum in, then cut the watermelon open and it's rotten? You've just wasted a bottle of rum."

"Hey, Tommy," I interrupted. "I did my last session ever today."

"Really?"

"Yeah. For real. I'm done."

"That's great! Right on, mama! What are you gonna do now?"

"I don't know. Pray. Learn a mantra and do it every day until I become a channel for infinite riches. I got an extra five hundred out of the bishop so I can coast for a little while. I'm just gonna apply everywhere and see if anyone will take me. Maybe I'll become an Avon Lady."

"Oh, Alice. I'm so proud of you, baby! Maybe we could both become Avon Ladies!"

"Or Mary Kay. They're kind of cooler."

"We could get matching pink Cadillacs."

Tommy put down the knife he was now using to cut open the watermelon and hugged me. He squeezed me so hard and happily that he lifted me in the air.

"We gotta celebrate," he said.

"I think we are celebrating. We've been celebrating all along."

"How do you feel?"

"Less tired and defeated than I have in two years. Less like I wanna kill myself or more like, if I'm gonna kill myself, I'll do it slowly, with Budweiser."

"It's really tough to kill yourself on domestic beer. Trust me. I've tried."

He sat down on the chartreuse velvet couch in my kitchen and cracked open two beers, handing me one as I sat down next to him.

"I hope you've been keeping journals because someday, someone is gonna wanna read this story and you are the one who should write it," he said. "The biggest danger of working in the sex industry is that you end up in someone else's shitty screenplay or novel. Don't let that happen to you. You don't want some dude writing your book."

"I'm not sure anyone will ever take me seriously. I write in a journal that says 'Supergirlistic' all over it and my last journal had kittens all over it. The one before that, a unicorn. I don't exactly feel like Hemingway."

"I'll bet Hemingway had a notebook with little kittens on it."

"He did love cats. Ones with six toes per paw especially."

"Listen, a writer friend of mine once told me that the two most important things required to write a good memoir are horrible shit has to happen to you, and you can't die."

"Hemingway is dead."

"Yeah, but he only bit the shit after he wrote some good stuff and his biting the shit was his own doing with his fave shotgun. And, p.s.—*You* are still alive."

"Yeah, but the horrible shit I've 'gone through' is all my own doing. It's shit I've gotten myself into."

"Well, now you've gotten yourself out of it so cheers to being alive."

We clinked Bud cans and took a couple large swigs.

"Where has your roommate been? I haven't seen Jake in so long I'm not really buying he still exists."

"Oh, Jake exists all right, but every time you've seen him in the last month, you've been drunk. And he's been staying at his new boyfriend's, taking acting classes and working sixty hours a week to pay for the acting classes so I hardly see him anymore."

"Whatever you say. I'm sure Mr. Snuffleupagus totally lives here."

"Do you know how upset it used to make me when only Big Bird could see Snuffleupagus? I was traumatized when Big Bird would say to everyone, 'No guys, seriously—He was right here!' And everyone on *Sesame Street* acted like he was crazy. They actually changed it recently so everyone could see Snuffleupagus because so many kids were having breakdowns over it."

"I never liked Big Bird. I liked Ernie but Bert was a fucking asshole."

"I liked the Count. He was Goth. And Oscar the Grouch."

"You know he's based on Diogenes? Going around in a garbage can, philosophizing."

"That makes sense. He always said the truth even if he pissed everyone off."

"I think I'm gonna start watching *Sesame Street* again. It's the best thing on TV."

"Isn't it on in the morning?"

"I have no idea."

Tommy and I stopped talking for a moment to sip more beer and flip through our internal TV Guides when he suddenly noticed my hairbrush sitting on the couch. It was the one Lord H had given me and it was full of hair, tangled mounds of my long brown tresses.

"Is that all your hair?" he asked, picking it up.

"Yeah. I get elf locks."

"What are elf locks?"

"When you sleep at night and elves climb onto your bed and tangle your hair up. Then in the morning it's a mess. It's kind of a mess right now."

"Lemme see."

He picked up the brush and combed it lightly through my hair, so lightly that it almost tickled. I sighed with pleasure and leaned further back while he continued brushing my hair. I wanted him to brush my hair forever. It was almost better than sex.

"You've got a lot of hair. While I get less hair, you seem to just get more."

"I'm Black Irish. We've got thick hair. Too bad it'll be gray by the time I'm 28."

"Well, it's great. It's like a waterfall or something."

"Hey, you wanna go up to my roof? I think the landlords left it unlocked."

"Let's do it. Soon enough it'll be too cold to go anywhere."

We grabbed our watermelon, our sporks, our beer, two folding beach chairs and my Hello Kitty boombox and took everything upstairs for some moonbathing. The moon was little more than a sliver and the night was clear enough you could almost see the stars.

My boombox was old, busted and covered in duct tape. Each time I put a CD into it, I had to tape the CD player closed lest it continually pop open. I taped a Hank Williams CD into it and we sat back in our folding chairs as Hank began to mournfully sing about a life of sin on the lost highway.

"I'm getting you a new CD player for your next birthday," Tommy said.

"I don't mind it. Everything I own is broken or taped up. My toaster oven, the microwave, my TV. Even the moon is broken tonight."

"It's just a shiny half. But it's all we got."

"Yeah. You can't really wish upon a star here since they're so hard to see you have to wish upon the moon, but then sometimes I think to ask the moon for something and then I feel bad because I have more than most people. Who am I to wish for anything? This morning, I was sitting on my stoop, drinking coffee and smoking a cig, just watching people go by and wondering how the world continues to function at all, and a father and his two sons walked by me. They all carried luggage and the father looked desperate and sad. The smallest boy, his backpack was broken and I wished someone would fix it for him. I wondered where the mother was and my mind immediately jumped to something tragic. If I could wish for anything it would be that those boys will be okay, that I could fix his bag or help him. I care more about those boys than I do myself."

"Me too. I couldn't care less about myself. I just kind of put up with myself."

"I put up with myself the way I put up with this Hello Kitty boombox. I can't be fixed, just taped up so I can keep playing the same sad country songs over and over."

"At least you can still be taped up. Some people can't."

I thought about what Tommy had done with the brush, lightly combing my hair with what had been an implement of torture. He was taping me up, reminding me that I could still feel and even more than that, he was reminding me that I could still feel *good*.

He continued, "I had one of those moments the other day—the moments where you see someone or something so sad that you just go—J*esus, who am I to complain about anything?* I was sitting waiting for the D Train and you know how that station is. It's like there are always people there, 24 hours a day. Chinese immigrants who you know just busted ass in some garment shop and they're coming home at two in the morning just to wake up and do it again. So I was sitting there and this poor Chinese guy who was clearly 'special needs' came up to me. He started telling me about a girl he was in love with who'd gone off to school. He missed her and wanted to write her a love letter and he'd been wandering around all night trying to get people to help him because he could barely write in English. I offered to help him and he had me write questions like 'Do you have a lot of homework?' and 'Do you like school?' The letter was already filled with all different types of handwriting so obviously other people had been helping him. Was just so fucking heartbreaking."

"Kind of makes you wonder who the girl is."

"Yeah. I wondered if she was also 'special needs.'"

"If she wasn't that almost makes it worse. Maybe she was a hooker."

"Well, it seemed pretty clear she's not coming back anytime soon."

"Damn, this watermelon is good."

I dug my spork into the watermelon and ate a big piece. It was sweet and crisp and I washed it down with a swig of Budweiser. The seeds I spit over the side of the roof. Doing so, I felt like Huck Finn hanging with Tom Sawyer. I felt like the tomboy I'd once been and still was.

"It's nice up here," Tommy observed. "Like a little nirvana."

"It's like Eden except you have to wear clothes unless you want the yuppies in that building with the big windows to see your junk. I should really just move up here and stop paying rent."

"Might be tough in the winter."

"It's tough in the winter anyway. If it weren't for my space heater, I'd freeze my ass clean off. I think my body is intended for tropical climates."

"Jesus, me too. If LA weren't the most terrible place on earth, I'd move there for the weather. I had this ex call the other day; if you could call someone I had a 3-week relationship with an ex. She just moved to LA and said, 'It's so great here. I walk into my backyard and grab a peach from one of the peach trees that grows there.' And, I said, 'When I want a peach, you know what I do? I walk to the bodega and I buy one.' That kinda threw a wrench into her little 'LA is great' speech. Here you just go to the bodega. Everything you could ever want is in this city. You wanna know the future? You go to the psychic a block away."

"You wanna forget the past, you go one of ten million bars within a five block radius. This city has everything you need and everything you want but shouldn't have."

"Or everything you want but can't have."

Tommy looked me square in the eyes. It was a look intended to communicate something—He wanted me, but he couldn't have me and the only reason he couldn't is because he believed I should possess the freedom to give myself completely to art. F. Scott Fitzgerald once wrote in a short story that a character had suddenly seen that, "…love was a big word like life and death." Tommy believed art was just as big, that it was integral to the survival of our species and he believed he and I were integral to art's survival, that once we got through our twenties, we would do great things.

I wasn't sure. I only knew that Tommy and I were like Zelda and F. Scott, but not as a couple. We were both comprised of equal parts Zelda and F. Scott. Whereas Zelda's insane behavior was almost always F. Scott's inspiration, our own individual insanity was our inspiration. We were our own Zeldas. To be your own Zelda is exhausting.

The Downtown skyline was glowing—the Twin Towers and the Woolworth building.

"I love the Woolworth Building," I said.

"Why?"

"Because I love Woolworth's."

"I can't believe they're all closing. So sad. Was like the only place where you could walk in empty-handed and walk out with a thigh-master, cheese curls, a sewing kit and a live parakeet."

"The 14th Street one already closed. I bought a red basket there for like two bucks. I wanted the whole lunch counter but it was over a thousand dollars."

"If I ever run for president, my entire platform is gonna be reopening Woolworth's."

"I'd vote for you."

"They're still gonna have Woolworth's in Mexico."

"Maybe we ought to move to Mexico. The Woolworth Building kind of looks like the Wizard's headquarters in Oz when you really look at it."

"So does the Empire State Building. That's how you know The Wizard of Oz was shot in the '30s. It's all 'deco.'"

"I love the Empire State Building, but you can't see it from here so sometimes it doesn't feel like Manhattan. You can only see downtown from here and I kind of like it like that. I wanna forget there's a world above 14th Street"

"Wait? There's a world above 14th Street? You know, Alice, this is my favorite building in New York."

"Really? It smells like ass, rodents the size of Chihuahuas live in the hallways and it's owned by the evilest piece of shit landlord on earth."

"Yeah, but every time I come here I get to see you."

"It's exasperating when you flirt with me, when you say things like that because then I wonder why we've never just gone for it, become boyfriend and girlfriend, gotten engaged, moved to Queens, started breeding and all that. I love you so much and yet, I endure the hell of dating others."

"Alice, marriage is for dull people."

"Well then, let's be dull. Seriously, why not? We have chemistry, love, like, shared opinions, no religion, political views, the same boundaries. You know I drank pee and you don't care. You love me anyway. I *want* to be dull. I *want* to be bored for once."

"We can't do it, Alice. You are sooooo young and I'm crazier than a shithouse condominium. And I'm terrified of intimacy. Did I ever tell you about Beep-Beep Dinosaur and Tee-Tee Chameleon?"

"Nope."

"They were my lizards when I was about seven. I used to go out into the backyard and collect potato bugs for them to eat, which I put in their cage. Then one morning, I woke up and the bugs had eaten Beep-Beep alive. The worst part wasn't even the carnage, it's that Tee-Tee had to witness the carnage. I don't think I've been able to forge a healthy relationship since. I'd always rather be Beep-Beep than Tee-Tee. I can't handle seeing anyone else in pain so I walk away before I have to. But you almost seem impervious to pain. Physical and mental."

"Not impervious, just numb."

I was tired of being numb. That night I wanted to *really* feel things, to be completely aware of everything, from Tommy's warm breath next to mine to the smell of Budwesier and watermelon to the soft, quiet darkness up on the roof and the approaching end of summer.

"Bad news, Alice is you'll never be dull and you'll never be bored. And if I thought I could ever have a hand in making you bored, I would run from you."

"Then what I want from you is simple. I need you to tell me everything is gonna be OK, as you've done for me so many times. I always need that reminder—the tunnel then the light, winter before spring, darkest before dawn because right now I need sunlight. I need warmth and fire and if I can't be dull with you, I need to burn the town down with you."

"That, I can do and if I'm ever not there, then you go outside for 10 minutes, close your eyes and feel the sun on your face. Remember that little stray kitten we saw sitting outside of the bodega?"

"I'll never forget that amazing little creature."

"Right. She was mangy, small, fighting for her survival, but she was sitting in the sunlight and just digging it. She was completely Zen. Her life was hard but she was in the right place at the right time and she knew it."

"She was ancient. Her eyes were anyway."

"That kitten was like you, an anomaly. Old and young, desperate but almost bathed in invisible jewels. She was a queen among cats and she was only a kitten."

Tommy looked up at the moon, thinking about the kitten, while I fiddled with the ring H had given me. Doing so always quieted my overactive monkey mind, but now it felt heavier. It was my only piece of jewelry and yet I hated everything it represented. I hated jewelry in general, the weight of it, the noise it made, the money it cost. It seemed like the most unnecessary thing in the world. I'd considered taking the H ring to a pawnshop and selling it, but I wanted nothing else from H, not a cent. With it on, I felt like Frodo carrying the One Ring. Each day that I wore it, I'd grown a little weaker, the bags under my eyes got a little bigger and my resolve to quit being his slave slowly vanished. Now, like Frodo and his ring, I had to get rid of the fucking thing. When Tommy went downstairs to fetch more beer, I stood up, walked to the edge of the roof and pitched the ring down into the alley. Maybe, if someone ever cleaned the alley, they'd find it under the piles of garbage, used condoms and empty Georgi bottles and they'd feel lucky. But, I felt lucky to be rid of it.

When Tommy returned, I didn't tell him what I'd just done. No one ever noticed the ring anyway. It wasn't a big piece of bling though my finger felt dramatically lighter without it.

We popped open two more cans of Bud and proceeded to do what we did best—talk for hours until the beer was almost gone, the moon began to vanish and the first light appeared in the sky. Eventually, it was dawn, a pink and purple sunrise with clouds that looked like Rubens had painted them. It was the dawn Tommy had promised me almost two years earlier.

## Chapter 33

## *Life Support*

By sunrise, Tommy and I were piss-drunk, but still wide awake and joyful. My twenties were an exercise in sleeplessness, in staying awake for fear I might miss something. Nowadays, twentysomethings get all kinds of good pills like Ambien and Xanax. Back then, we only had booze and it didn't always do the trick. We grabbed the lawn-chairs and boombox and headed back downstairs. Jake was coming out of the bathroom buck-naked just as we walked in—a Lower East Side *Three's Company* moment. He quickly cupped his hand over his penis. His other hand gripped a bagel.

"I got bagels, you guys," he said, slurring his words. "I've discovered they're way fresher when I get them on my way home from The Cock at five in the morning."

He took a bite out of his bagel, staggered into his bedroom, closed the door and passed out, likely with the bagel still in his hand. I often did the same with falafel only to wake up with ground chickpeas and cucumber sauce in my hair.

Tommy and I wandered into my bedroom. I wasn't necessarily horny, but I didn't want him to go. We kissed. His entire tongue went into my mouth and felt its way around. He pulled it out and we kissed sweetly. His breath went into my breath. My breath went into his. It was like we were giving each other CPR—resuscitation for the not actually dying—CPR for the living, or rather, the dying slowly. Life support for those who wish they'd never been born.

In an instant his boxer briefs were down ever so slightly and I could see that the tip of his penis was hard. I gently licked it, while slipping my jeans off. He pulled the Yoda t-shirt over my head and licked my nipples.

"What do you want, baby?" he asked. "Tell me what you want."

"Can you take my pain away? Tall order, I know."

"I'll do what I can."

A black, chiffon scarf I got from Woolworth's was sitting next to my bed. Sometimes I wore it jauntily tied around my neck like Laverne on *Laverne and Shirley*. He picked it up, smiling.

"Come here, sweetheart,'" he said.

He shoved the scarf into my mouth then wrapped it tightly around my head, tying it at the front of my face. He leaned over and pressed his lips to my now-gagged mouth.

"Part of me thinks you liked the things you did at the dungeon but you hated the men you did it with."

I wanted to respond vocally but couldn't. Instead, my body responded with wetness, with a desire that made me dizzy.

"Get on your stomach," he said.

Grabbing the excess fabric of the scarf, he tied it to an eyehook jutting out from the wall, a few inches from my bed. The hook was a souvenir from the one time Stu and I had toyed with bondage. My face was now bound to the wall's surface and I was fairly immobilized. He took hold of my hair and pulled my head upwards. Kissing the side of my face sweetly, he then pulled away in order to fully undress. When he was finished I felt his naked body press up against mine. The gag cut into me slightly and the fabric smelled like a musky combination of dried saliva and burnt nylon. His growing erection pressed against my leg as he caressed my ass with his hands. Moaning, I thrust my ass toward the heavens and toward him.

"I like it when you make those noises," he said, reaching between my legs and slipping two fingers into my dripping pussy. He thrust them in and out, stroking my g-spot until I was on the brink of climax.

"Don't come yet," he said, pulling his fingers out to unwrap a condom.

I maneuvered upwards and spread my thighs further apart. He guided his cock into my pussy and began to fuck me hard.

"Don't come yet," he said again, pulling out of me and quickly untying the gag. He then rolled me onto my back and pulled his condom off at which point I took his cock in my mouth, first the tip and then the shaft. I gazed at his wiry, pale body then looked into his big, brown eyes.

"You look gorgeous right now," he said, gently stroking my hair as I continued to give him head. After several minutes, he again told me to turn onto my stomach, which I did. Then, using the black scarf, he tied my wrists together and tied them to the eyehook on the wall. He ran his tongue down my neck and bit me playfully.

"Please fuck me again," I gasped. "Please," I said again as I heard him unwrap another condom.

He slid the condom on and grabbed a bottle of Astroglide sitting on my windowsill—another souvenir from my time with Stu. He warmed a glob of it between his palms. I knew what this meant and my asshole, as usual, tightened up in fear.

"Relax," he said.

"Please go slow," I begged.

"I will."

And with that, he thrust his cock inside my asshole. Since my hands were bound there was little I could do to prevent this from happening so I tried to relax. Turns out, I was so turned on that my body readily accepted him and I actually began to enjoy it. I thought about what Dylan said on my first day at the dungeon—*It's not like doing it for love.* Now I was tied up, taking it in the ass and really, truly enjoying it because I *was* doing it with someone I loved, trusted and respected, who respected me and understood that my time clothed and thinking was just as valuable as my time naked and fucking.

As I rocked back and forth on Tommy's cock, he reached into my bedside nightstand and pulled out my vibrating dildo, the crazy tiki-doll faced one he and Kyle had given me. Tommy knew everything about me, including where I kept my vibrator and how much I loved it. He turned it on high, reached around and pressed the little polar bear-shaped clitoral stimulator against my clit at which point, my body completely relaxed.

"You can go faster," I said. "Faster and deeper."

He did as suggested while using a free hand to work

the vibrating dildo inside of me. My entire body was contracting—my asshole around his penis, my cunt around the dildo.

"I can feel it vibrating," Tommy noted. "It feels amazing."

"Fuck, Tommy. I'm about to come." I couldn't hold off for another second.

"Come, baby. Come all over me," he said and I responded by doing just that, drenching the crazy dildo, the sheets and probably the mattress beneath it, if not the very inner core of Planet Earth. A few seconds later, Tommy came too.

The sun shone brightly through my chintzy pink curtains. Most regular people were probably waking up to go to work. Tommy pulled the dildo out of me and brought his hand to my mouth. I kissed his fingers and sucked on his hand as we rocked back and forth.

"I love you," I mumbled incoherently.

"I love you," he said, his cock still planted firmly in my asshole.

He pulled out slowly and untied my wrists.

"That might be the most I've ever come in my life," he noted, slipping the condom off.

"Me too. Ugh. That sun is too bright. Everything hurts."

"Agreed. It needs to be night again."

"I wish it could be the hours between happy hour and last call forever."

"I wish I could be in your bed forever."

"We could pull a John and Yoko."

"What have we got to protest?"

"Everything."

## Chapter 34

## *My Sun*

Maybe you wanted me to fall in love at the end of this book, for some knight in shining armor to swoop in and save me. That's what I wanted or at least what I *thought* I wanted, but it didn't happen. No one swooped in or saved me. No one did anything I can't do for myself except maybe fuck me (though it could be argued that I'm great at fucking myself, that I've fucked myself over and over again with terrible life choices.) But, in the end, I had to stop fucking myself. I had to swoop in. I had to save myself. I loved Tommy, but we didn't fall "in love" with each other. Our love never became an elevated form of insanity. Instead, we loved each other enough to protect one another's sanity. We gave each other room to grow, to be young, free and stupid. That might be the truest love there is. It's not passionless, but it's not possessive either. It's like pre-Global Warming weather. No ice caps melt. Everything is as it should be, not so terrifying or apocalyptic. It's not the kind of love that'll pull your house up into the air and take you to Oz on a crazy new adventure. It's more like the end of the adventure where you realize you don't have to look any further than your own backyard where all your friends are hanging out. So much attention gets paid to love and sex that friendship hardly gets noticed. There aren't many fairytales about friendship. Love, Life and Death are big words but what so often gets overlooked is just having someone to call when things are tough.

What happened in all the fairytales and Disney Movies the world shoved down my childhood throat simply didn't happen in real-life adulthood. Rats weren't gonna sew me a gown and Fairy Godmothers weren't gonna come to my rescue. Certainly, after what I'd witnessed in the sex industry, a man would not come to my rescue. The teakettle and saucer weren't gonna talk and neither were the walls. Thank Christ.

The thing that did save me, that did talk, was the thing that almost killed me—desperation. I was desperate to be free of the industry and of the feeling that I could be bought and sold. This meant pounding the pavement with my ridiculous fake résumé until I landed a crap job at Barnes and Noble, earning little more than minimum wage. In outfits fit for a librarian, I rang up books and prayed I wouldn't come face to face with any former clients. For years, I prayed I wouldn't run into clients until I forgot what most of them looked like. I think if I saw H today, I wouldn't recognize him.

Tommy and I spent a lot of nights like the one spent on my roof and a lot of early hours like the one spent in my bed. I learned to enjoy loving S&M, specifically with him. I was a true submissive but I also appreciated gentleness. I appreciated *kissing*, the one thing I hardly ever did at the dungeon. I appreciated falling asleep next to someone, listening to his heartbeat and wondering what he were dreaming about.

Being with Tommy, especially making love to him was like getting sunburned. I felt it for days afterward and remembered the sun that gave it to me—that sun being Tommy—sometimes too bright, too harsh and too much but always, he was my warmth, the emergency energy generator that kept me going when the lights went out because he did the one thing I asked of him—he told me everything would be okay even when it was clearly gonna be rough. He always reassured me the dawn would come though he never lied to me about the chaos that might come with it. And he fulfilled his other promise of never having a hand in making me dull or bored even when I begged for boredom and stability. Even as I write this, many years after the first time we made love, neither of us has settled down, had a family or moved to Queens. Tommy is successful now. He's lived all over the world, but never in Queens or any other place where he might risk having a lawn. He and I never became an item and for that I'm glad. I never want to be part of anything considered an "item" just as I never want to be considered an "object." I only ever want to be human—sometimes failing, sometimes succeeding, sometimes foolish but always feeling.

The cane marks faded a few days after I quit and, as far as I know, the ring is still buried under piss and filth in the alley. The hairbrush, I threw out and the mary janes and schoolgirl uniform, I gave to the Salvation Army. I often wonder where they ended up. In fact, I wonder where they ended up more than I wonder where most of my clients ended up. Just as the men I saw couldn't have cared less what happened to me once my Lolita days ended, I hardly ever thought about them except while writing this book.

My job hawking books lasted less than a year and was followed by several other crap retail jobs. After quitting the sex industry, I had almost as many day jobs as I'd had clients. I continued to send out pornographic essays and eventually *Penthouse Variations* picked up one story. They asked me to tone down the violence of the sex so it could be sold and read in Canada where everyone is nice and sex can't be depicted as being too mean or harsh. It wasn't exactly like writing for Vanity Fair but it paid four hundred dollars, about as much as I'd earned doing sessions. And it gave me confidence that I was on my way to having some sort of career as a writer. What kind of career it would be, I couldn't say, only that I felt certain it would happen.

## Chapter 35

## *Little Bird*

A few months after my last session I decided, for the first time in my life, to try therapy. After all I'd done and seen I was pretty sure I needed it. I bore no visible scars from the dungeon but the invisible ones were lingering far past their due date. My nerves were shot to shit. My sleep was plagued with nightmares and my soul hurt like a motherfucker. Making art helped, but the second I put down my pen or paintbrush, I grew anxious. It was if my entire being was comprised of equal parts panic, anxiety, low self-esteem, hypomania and Budweiser.

Given my new line of work, scraping together forty bucks for the initial intake at the National Institute for the Psychotherapies wasn't easy but I deemed it necessary. I was told a therapist could see me Wednesday at 9:30. This would mean taking the subway—a terrifying ordeal for someone who'd been out of the real world for so long—during rush hour.

I hopped on the F and it was a hot, sweaty mess, not in a good way. Panic seemed imminent, but I pressed on, hoping to get to 57th Street without a freak-out. I stood. I sat. I tried to read *Star*. Couldn't focus so I stood back up, sat back down, wash, rinse, repeat and feel crazy. At 42nd

Street, propelled by a little voice inside my head that said, "Get the fuck off the train NOW," I did just that. I would be late, but hell—it's therapy! Seems like the one thing it's okay to be a little late for.

I walked up Broadway in the sunshine past the hordes of tourists in statue of liberty foam headgear and businesspeople in suits and I noticed these people noticing something. "Aww," I heard a few say. They then made sad faces and moved on. I looked down.

In the middle of the sidewalk on Broadway between 42nd and 43rd, there were two birds. One was lying on its back seemingly injured. It looked like it was dying but there was no blood. It was twitching around like it had a wing injury and it opened and closed its beak letting out barely audible noises. The other was hovering over it, wanting to help but seeing as how it didn't have any opposable thumbs, there was shit all it could do. It just watched helplessly as its friend struggled. They were plump little birds. They almost looked like titmice though I don't know if there are titmice in Times Square. They looked young like they'd just shed their baby bird down for real feathers. Maybe they'd just left the nest and made their first outing into the "real world" only to discover that the world is dangerous and full of uncaring assholes.

I considered moving on too. Again, I was late for therapy! But how much therapy would I need if I *did* walk on? I would TRY to do something. Better to try and fail than not try at all. One of my many favorite mottos and one of the reasons I fail constantly.

Remembering I had a towel I'd stolen from the YMCA in my bag, I knelt down. The other bird flew away, knowing I had thumbs and knowing I would do something. Using the stolen towel I gently cupped the bird's tiny possibly titmouse adolescent body in my hands. All the people who were previously rushing by began to pause and watch what was happening. As carefully as humanly possible, I turned the bird over and placed it on its feet. I expected the worst—that it would keel over and die. Instead, it took a second to muster some strength then triumphantly flew away, high above the Great White Way and over the heads of all the people who'd just walked on by. Hopefully it went to meet its friend. Maybe they went off to Rudy's for a pint. Maybe I would join them later. Maybe, even though I am comprised of panic, anxiety, low self-esteem, hypomania and Budweiser, I am not really that fucked up. Maybe I just want the world to be gentler than it is.

I put the stolen towel back in my bag and stood up. A weathered old truck driver who'd been watching the whole thing from his truck gave me a thumbs up. It felt good, so good I considered blowing off therapy. After all, maybe I wasn't the one who needed therapy; maybe all the people who walked by the suffering bird did. Or maybe I needed therapy precisely *because* I lived in a world where people noticed a suffering bird and did nothing to help. In the end, I decided to go to therapy because like that bird, I just needed someone to help me get back on my feet.

The therapist was young, female and genuinely fascinated by my crazy life. It felt good to simply blather for an hour while also admitting things I'd kept locked away in journals or only told to my closest friends.

"This might be too much information," I said at one point.

"There's no such thing here," she responded.

That's when I knew I loved therapy. Sadly, I could only afford three more sessions before reality kicked in via a Con Ed bill marked "final notice" in bold, red letters. Mental stability is important, but electricity more so.

I remembered what an open mike performer who'd recently been booted from the psych ward at Bellevue once said onstage—"When you're rich you're bipolar. When you're poor, you're just fucked up."

And I was fucked up, barely able to function in the normal world and therefore too broke for therapy. But the incident with the bird showed me something more valuable than therapy. I was fucked up—I was a drunk who continually made terrible life choices, who'd been a prostitute and was now a pornographer, but I was also the one person who stopped for that little bird. I was the one person that morning who didn't take beauty and life for granted. It was not only what made me an artist; it was what made me human.

## *Epilogue*

More than fifteen years have passed since I first stepped foot in a dungeon. At the beginning of this book I write that I don't regret anything I've done. That's true mostly because regret is a waste of time. You can sit around bemoaning all the stupid shit you've done and the bad decisions you've made or you can reflect on the stupid shit and the bad decisions and realize they've made you a wiser, more compassionate human being, one who is less likely to judge lest ye be judged. Putting this book out there means I'll be judged. If I'm lucky, a zealot will burn it and I'll make millions. No doubt I'll be called a whore, which is okay. Whores are beautiful. Hypocrites are not. And someday, I'll go to my grave knowing I was never a hypocrite.

In writing this book, I've self-reflected to a point of exhaustion, turned the manuscript into a slightly fictitious novel (for various reasons, mostly legal) and wondered, probably as many times as you have while reading this, *"What the fuck was she thinking?"* In hindsight I realize that there were other options I could have explored as a broke twenty-three-year old, but I didn't. Why I didn't, I'll never know. I do know that I chose to traverse a pretty dark road, one where I saw the darkness in others and I explored the darkness in myself. Maybe it truly was writer's curiosity that led me down this path. At the end of the day, I got a whole lot more "material" than I'd bargained for—something I now consider a gift. I experienced excruciating pain and occasional sexual ecstasy while also getting a firsthand look at the fetishes, obsessions and desires of grown men. I realized that some had to sexualize the horrors of their past just to deal with the present while others were simply bored, kinky or curious. And I was the receptacle for their horrors, their boredom, their kinks and their curiosity. I eventually realized that I was *not* Alice falling down the rabbit hole; I was the other side of the looking glass. I was a world different from the one that had failed them. I was always told the body was a temple and that prostitution was a sort of desecration of this temple, but I now believe prostitutes are often the only temples where a man can find peace.

*Acknowledgments*

This book wouldn't have been possible without several bad life decisions and the help of many people. To name just a few: Thank you, Bruce Ronn, for encouraging me to forgo the regular publishing process and take a D.I.Y. approach. Together we are starting "Art Star Scene Press" wherein we will print things that are actually underground and maybe save the last vestiges of bohemia from hipster entrapment. Thanks to Marie Mundaca for designing the book, copyediting and doing technical things I am incapable of. Thanks to Ann Enzminger Bronshav for the cover photo, to Joe Heaps Nelson for editing and to Scooter Pie for reading and rereading the manuscript, offering me encouragement and courage to put my work out there on my own. Thanks to Dylan Greenberg for the adorable ASS Press logo and to David Dyte for additional editing Life is maddening at times, but the following friends have helped me see the light at the end of the tunnel. Christine Colby, my editor at *Penthouse,* who's published a few of the essays herein, has shown me there's a mass market for edgy smut. Various friends who've supported my work over the years and given me endless stories, some of which are recounted and fictionalized here, are countless. Without Faceboy and his open mike, I would likely not be a writer. Without his love, I wouldn't be here. Without Jeff Kenny, Lorne, Tom Tenney and J-Boy, I would have never laughed so hard during tough times and had so many stories to tell. Velocity Chyaldd was instrumental in teaching me to "own" my depravity and to be proud of what I am no matter what others think. And venues like Collective Unconscious and Surf Reality, now lost to greedy landlordism, gave me a platform where I could openly say and do things that aren't considered the norm. So many other people to thank including Robert Prichard, Kat Green, Kellie Burke, Courtney Webber, Jonathan Ames, John Foster, all of the art stars and more. Whether you like it or not, you helped this book happen.